Northern Hemisphere
Southern Hemisphere

Northern Hemisphere Southern Hemisphere

The Power of Love

Claudia Compagnucci

Balboa Press books may be ordered through booksellers or by contacting:

Balboa Press
A Division of Hay House
1663 Liberty Drive
Bloomington, IN 47403
www.balboapress.com
1 (877) 407-4847

Print information available on the last page.

ISBN: 978-1-5043-3166-1 (sc)
ISBN: 978-1-5043-3168-5 (hc)
ISBN: 978-1-5043-3167-8 (e)

Library of Congress Control Number: 2015906283

Balboa Press rev. date: 7/1/2015

Dedicated to:
RI.DR.

Contents

Acknowledgments

I would like to thank my American coach, Jill Cahill. Thank you for your words and support, Jill. Your strength and motivation are incredible! I also thank everyone in Jack Canfield's team, especially Josiah Barlow because he unconditionally believed in me. Thank you for your music, Josiah! I'd especially like to thank Jack Canfield for all I have learned from him. His focus and pragmatism can generate a special dynamic in his trainees; he helps people find their inner strength and realize their full potential. Thanks to Mark Moffitt from Bob Proctor's team for your support and advice. You have helped me understand the meaning of the word *determination*.

I would also like to thank certain people who contributed to my work by special meaningful coincidences, probably without being aware of having helped me: Valeria and Alejandra, who introduced me to Deepak Chopra's literature, and Helvia and María José. Special thanks to Sonia, Brenda, Mo, Bea, and Joe.

Thank you to my family. To my father, Juan, you have shown me the value and balance of looking at the positive side of things that take place in people's lives. Thanks to my mother, Inés, who has always been with us and still is. Thank you to Laura, Lucas, Ricardo, and Cristina! Angela, thank you!

Thank you to my best friends Ana and Susana, Ana María, Andrea, and Adriana. My "Mastermind Group" at Canfield Coaching: Valina in Great Britain; Gaby in México, Joyce in Ireland, and Neena in India.

A special and deep thanks to my children: Hernán and Brenda. I am proud of your balance, integrity, and adultness under any circumstance. I know you are remarkable people. I love you!

The Author's Words

My goal with this book is to help people understand that meaningful coincidences exist. They can happen to any of us—and they *do*. But if we do not believe they are possible, we will probably miss the chance to change our lives or elevate them to a different conscious level of understanding.

I am not only writing this to tell an amazing love story, a story that may have profound meaning to some people and be just another love story to others. I would also like to leave a message for those who are capable of listening—in the deepest and most intense sense of the word. Listening to all of those phrases we usually ignore just because we are using our senses. That is to say: we *hear* but we do not *listen*. I would like whoever reads this book to halt, to stop, to lower the rhythm, and to listen to the people around you. There might be a message that could change some circumstance in your life.

Listen to what is beyond the words.

Listen to what transcends the boundaries of their meaning and becomes a message from the soul.

Claudia Compagnucci

Introduction

Coincidences

- Space: Buenos Aires, Argentina
- Time: 2007

Clara was a tall, beautiful middle-aged woman who lived in Buenos Aires. She worked as an English teacher in a company. Six years had passed since she got divorced, and life had not been easy for her since then.

The sun was shining brightly one afternoon. Clara had given a lesson and was walking along a sidewalk looking for a place to have lunch. She peacefully followed the people in front of her. Clara was window shopping when she suddenly found herself standing at the entrance of a large book shop on Santa Fe Avenue in Palermo. The title of a book by Deepak Chopra called out to her as she recalled a conversation she had had at work with a colleague two years before.

It was 2005 when she had first heard the idea that certain coincidences were signs from the universe. These signs could manifest in the form of a message sent to you by someone who was no longer here or they could reveal themselves through something written in a magazine, newspaper, or leaflet; they could even be something heard on television or seen in a movie. Clara's colleague Alexandra had introduced her to this subject one day when they were sharing a coffee together at work.

They had been talking about love. Alex asked Clara about her life, and Clara told her something anyone would think was hard to understand; it was something kind of magical that had taken place some months before. After hearing the details, Alexandra said, "I have a piece of paper I tore from a section of a newspaper not long ago that simply explains what you are telling me now. I will bring it on Monday. You must read it."

The weekend was long as Clara anxiously waited for Monday to read what Alex wanted to share with her. When they met again at work, Alex gave her an old, untidily torn sheet of newspaper with an article about coincidences, time, space, and meaningful facts that take place in people's lives. She read that we do not generally pay attention to these kinds of signs, which tend to show us a way to follow or a message to guide us.

This was exactly what had happened to Clara. The piece of paper clearly explained what had stunned her some months before, in early 2005. And there was Alex bringing this text to her as a confirmation of a coincidence. Why had Clara told her? Why had she told Alex and not someone else? Was it a meaningful coincidence that she ended up sharing this event with Alex, who—without being aware—had a message for Clara written in an article she had kept? It was a pity the newspaper article did not have the author's name.

Alex and Clara did not know anything about one another. They had met at work a year before and didn't even share the same timetable. Alex taught Spanish to foreigners in the morning, and Clara taught English to employees in the afternoon. There was a short span of time at midday when they saw each other in the corridors. And that year there were two days a week when they shared a half-hour break at the same place in that big company.

Alexandra found this coincidence so amazing that she decided to give Clara the newspaper article as a present. Clara accepted it, thanked her, and kept it as a treasure.

- Space: Vicente López, Buenos Aires, Argentina.
- Time: 2007

Two years went by. Clara had a new job where she met another colleague, and events were repeated as if destiny were guiding her toward that person. This person was going to give her the key to explain, in a deeper way, the meaning of the article Alex had given her two years before.

Clara and Barbara, her new coworker, had many conversations about interesting subjects. One thing they talked about was coincidence, as well as time and space convergence. Barbara seemed to have a deep knowledge of these topics, and when Clara told her the same story she had told Alexandra two years before, Barbara asked her, "Have you ever read Deepak Chopra's books?" Clara had not. She did not even know who he was—this famous doctor and writer from India, who lived in the United States.

All of a sudden she heard Barbara saying, "You must read *Synchrodestiny* by Deepak Chopra." And she continued, "You cannot miss the chance of learning from his wisdom. Promise me you are going to read it."

Now Clara was standing in front of the bookshop window recalling her conversation with Barbara. The book there attracted her like a magnet and she was drawn inside the store. She took the book off the shelf and had a quick look inside before paying for it. To her surprise, she found that the beginning of Chopra's book *Synchrodestiny* had the same words that were written in the article Alexandra had given her two years before: *When we live taking into account meaningful coincidences, we connect to the subjacent field of infinite possibilities. Here starts the magic. This is a state I call synchrodestiny, where the spontaneous fulfillment of all our wishes is possibly achieved.* (Chopra, 2007)

It was amazing! Now she knew who had written that article! And the explanation for all these coincidences could be clearly understood by reading the book. She could hardly believe what was going on. She felt shocked and blessed to have discovered this and to have experienced meaningful coincidences herself—not only with her two coworkers, but also with what had happened to her at the beginning of 2005 regarding her love story.

Chapter 1

Space and Time Converge

This is a love story, a story that explains how the union of space and time can influence our lives. A story of messages from the soul, of union in spite of separation, of eternal love in spite of a long time and distant spaces.

- Space: Clara´s living room, Buenos Aires, Argentina.
- Time: February 2005.

Clara and Stella had finished their second university careers and were working together on a project. They were planning to create training courses for teachers. Clara was forty-two years old, but she looked younger; she had a fit body and dark hair that usually caught people's attention as it made her look naturally sexy. Stella was about fifty and had a pretty face. She was a clever woman with a strong personality.

Clara's living room had a soft, delicate, and refined fragrance that created a cozy and welcoming ambience. There was a fireplace that was not on, since the summer sun was quite hot in the southern hemisphere in February. The air conditioning refreshed the room.

Clara loved details, and her living room showed her personality. Anybody who entered her house for the first time was captivated by the essence of the décor. Every corner of the space reflected who she was. Although the house was very comfortable, it didn't have the snob factor or show signs of wealth. Indeed, Clara was not rich; she had to work hard to make a living. But the house was really beautiful, decorated in soft pastel colors that stood out against an entire wall painted in tones of blue. Against it, reflections of the lights carefully placed in different corners of the room made the space inviting and relaxing.

That day, Stella was telling Clara about something that had been worrying her. She was not comfortable with her feelings toward a man she had been dating for some months. She seemed to be in love, but at the same time she felt incomplete. She felt that a decision had to be made, but her ambivalence was not letting her think objectively.

"I don't know what to do," Stella said. "Perhaps I should see a psychic, someone to guide me, someone to help me."

"Wait a minute," Clara answered anxiously. "I once went to see a graphologist whom I was told was a fortune teller. She predicted several things that years later happened with a strange precision. For example, she foretold my wedding date within a three month's range, and this happened more than six years before I got married, when I had no idea I would. She also said my hand was marked with traveling lines. I'm going upstairs to look for a little box where I kept memories from times when I was single, I think I have this woman's address there"

Clara ran briskly up the stairs. She started searching inside the little box, which was full of papers. She was sure she had a card with the telephone or address she was looking for. Suddenly, she saw an envelope she recognized. She picked it up, turned it over, and noticed that inside it was a sheet of paper torn from a spiral notebook. It was a letter she had received seventeen years earlier.

Clara opened the envelope and began to read. When she reached the fourth line, she realized she could not continue reading due to the tears in her eyes. An enormous, profound emotion beyond description overcame her. She was reading—or trying to read—the letter Daniel had written to her before she married someone else. With tears rolling down her eyes and the sheet of paper in her hand, she went downstairs and said to Stella, "I am sorry, but I couldn't find the address."

Stella looked at her, astonished. Clara was crying while she said this, which obviously didn't make much sense.

"What is wrong? Why are you crying?" Stella asked.

"I didn't find the address, but look at what I have found," murmured Clara.

Clara began to read Daniel's letter she had kept for so long. The paper had turned somewhat yellow after seventeen years.

- Space: Buenos Aires, Argentina.
- Time: 25 years before.

It was Sunday morning. Daniel was at his house in Martinez. He woke up, went to the bathroom, showered, got dressed, splashed some cologne around his neck, and drank some coffee in a hurry. His mother could not believe he was up so early on a Sunday.

"I'm off, old girl," he said warmly.

"And where are you going so early on a Sunday?" she asked in surprise.

"I have a lesson with Clara, Mum."

"Today?"

"Yes, Mum. Bye!"

He got on his motorbike as fast as he could and disappeared around the corner. He was wearing black boots, jeans, and a white T-shirt that was flickering in the wind. He looked very handsome. His blue eyes shone under his dark brown hair.

"This boy is going to drive me crazy," mumbled his mother. "One day he says he is not going to study, that he doesn't care about school, and then he wakes up early on a Sunday and dashes off to take a lesson."

Daniel was sixteen years old. He lived with his mother and two brothers in a beautiful neighborhood north of Buenos Aires. Daniel was the youngest, and his parents had divorced when he was a little boy. He did not like to study, but there was something that drew him to these English lessons. He turned around the corner with his red Zanella and could see the park square in front of Clara's house. He reached it in a flash and immediately rang the bell. Clara was waiting for him.

"Hello, Daniel. How are you?" she said with a big smile.

When he entered the house, he remembered the day he had asked Clara to help him study for an exam he had to take, as he had previously failed the subject at school. In time he would realize he had fallen in love with her at first sight.

"Hello, Clara," said Daniel.

"How was your week?" she asked, showing interest.

"Fine, I had a fight with two or three, but at least I was let out," he answered.

Daniel was a boarder at a school during the week and went home on the weekends. Therefore, his lessons had to be on Saturdays and sometimes Sundays. The lesson was always long, and time flew for both Clara and Daniel.

Once the lesson was over, they would get into long conversations in which they laughed and told each other about their lives. He would ask her for advice, and she would listen. They had a passionate exchange of ideas that they both enjoyed.

She was two years older than Daniel, but he was a profound person who was interested in many things. He spent almost a whole year of lessons and interesting chats with Clara. They had friends in common, and they had already met at some friends' meetings before, where they became very close friends.

Clara was just trying to help her friend with some difficulties he had with the language. They both kept their intense mutual attraction secret from each other. It was an attraction based on a profound and philosophical connection of their souls—a connection that magically united them.

- Space: Mendoza province / Buenos Aires province. Argentina.
- Time: 1981.

Time was moving, acquiring rhythm, circulating. A year later, Daniel went to live in Mendoza. He and Clara started writing letters to each other. But the following year, Clara met a young man who invited her out. Simultaneously—and in a convergence of time and space fueling destiny with vibrations—Daniel arrived from Mendoza. He invited Clara out the day before she was going to go out with another man, without knowing of her other plans. It was as if someone had warned him that he could lose her, as if he wanted to leave a mark on her, a seal of ownership. This feeling was unconscious, of course. Why would he want *ownership* over Clara if he didn't know she was going to start a relationship with another man? They only became aware of this fact years later when they analyzed the confluence of events in their lives.

As Daniel was two years younger than Clara, he saw her as a goddess. He was a bit shy, and deep in his heart he was afraid of being rejected. But he summoned up the courage and invited her out for a coffee. It was a Friday evening, and he went by to pick her up. They went to a small coffee shop on the Avenida del Libertador in La Lucila called Gstaad My Love where they spent several hours chatting. Daniel told Clara he had plans to settle in Mendoza, a province by the Andes mountain range over one thousand kilometers away from Buenos Aires. At that moment she felt she was losing him. She hoped he would kiss her when they said goodbye, or perhaps in the car. Instead, he loaned her his jacket because it was cold, and in the car he turned the cassette player on. It began playing the Barbara Streisand song "Woman in Love." His best strategy was to ask her to translate the lyrics, and she began to do so, reciting in Spanish the love words in the song. Neither of them noticed the premonitory message in the lyrics:

I am a woman in love ... In love there is no measure of time ... We may be oceans away ... You feel my love, I hear what you say.

Clara repeated the words without knowing that destiny would separate her and Daniel. Daniel was ecstatic as he listened to the words he wanted to hear from the love of his life, not knowing he had chosen a song with the exact words destined for both of them.

That was the last time they would meet before he returned to Mendoza, but they would continue to be in touch and write even more letters to each other.

As he had finished school that year, he would continue his studies at university. He was planning to become an engineer. He surely went out, had fun, grew up, and perhaps fell for other women.

Clara, on the other hand, continued dating the young man she had gone out with the day after seeing Daniel. She also experienced a terrible tragedy, a violent and unexpected loss; sometimes the space-time convergence is unfortunate, and cruelly casts pain on people's lives. Clara's boyfriend's sister was run over by a bus when crossing the street. She was only eleven years old. It was a tragedy that left her boyfriend devastated and depressed. The loss wasn't his first; he had also lost his mother when he was born.

After several years of tremendous suffering due to this tragic loss, Clara and her boyfriend decided to get married. Clara loved her boyfriend and wanted to help him. She remained close to him, helping him recover. She was so overwhelmed by sadness that she didn't realize how much her deep love for Daniel had been growing inside her. They had such a special communication—even though it was only manifested by the letters they wrote to each other as friends. Daniel had not dared to kiss her the day they had gone out for coffee. However, they would realize in the future that his asking her to translate the lyrics of that song would have an even more powerful effect on their lives. At the time, they could not even imagine the reason he had chosen that specific song. Was there a hidden purpose behind this event? Was there a sign or a message hidden in the lyrics? Was there a coincidence surrounding their lives?

Word of Clara's engagement got around to family, friends, and acquaintances. The news reached Daniel, who had stopped writing sometime after the tragic events in Clara's life. He felt he was losing her, as she had grown so much closer to her boyfriend after the tragedy. Daniel felt it wasn't a good idea to interfere with her relationship during such a sad time. Maybe he realized how much he loved her and didn't think it would be fair to profit from such a situation to get close to her in any way. Deep in his heart, Daniel was shy. He felt he had nothing to offer her but his love. He was too young to realize that this was the most important thing.

With time and experience, Daniel would learn that when young people don't always realize that material things can be obtained if you need them or want them. But whatever is related to the *meaning* or the *intention* in our lives is the real reason we are here. So, material things are necessary, but they are not the most important ingredients in our lives. He would learn that discovering that meaning can take anyone years. Many of us need almost our whole lives to realize the profound meaning of our being here. And some people never realize what they have come here for, what the real meaning in their lives is.

Finally, after some time, Daniel started writing again. He was kind with his choice of words. He wanted to support her, knowing that she was going through a hard period in her life. He wanted to help her the same way she had helped him when he had been devastated by his father's death some years before. Daniel wrote letters that reflected his deep values and a philosophy that was very much in alignment with hers. He also never missed the opportunity to send her a joke or something to make her laugh. They were connected through a kind of energy that transcended the distance between them. They felt close to each other, even though they were not actually beside one another.

Some years went by. It was October 1987. One day, Daniel suddenly arrived in Buenos Aires from Mendoza and called Clara. He asked her to start English lessons again, and for a short period of time they met at her house for the lessons.

Approximately three months before her wedding, just before the end of a lesson, Daniel gave Clara a letter written in English. He asked her to read it when she had time and to correct it. With the excuse that he was in a hurry, he said he would leave it with her to be discussed at the following lesson. Clara was surprised with the contents of the letter; it was clear evidence of what was coming ahead in their lives. At that moment, they did not know what it meant. They could not even imagine that the lyrics of the song he had asked her to translate long before when they went out for coffee had been hiding a message. They would discover it almost seventeen years later.

Each word Daniel used in his letter was a manifestation of his feelings for her. There was something they couldn't imagine at that moment—something hidden behind those words.

December 8, 1987. In the letter, Daniel confessed his love for Clara and he suggested she run away with him.

The letter started like this: *This story is my story of impossible love … She is the most beautiful woman in the world.*

And it ended with the following phrase:

If you love me, will you come away with me?

Clara was stunned. She had always been attracted to Daniel, but she never imagined that he loved her so and had kept it a secret all this time.

She always felt he had a strong power over her—something difficult to explain because they had never even kissed—but now it was quite clear that they had desired each other.

Clara felt deep sorrow in her soul, knowing she could not abandon her boyfriend after all they had been through; plus, their wedding was only three months away. She had to draw on all her inner strength to face the situation and repress the desire and temptation to consider this crazy adventure of eloping and leaving all behind. She felt she could not do that to her boyfriend because she loved him.

Daniel's letter opened the door to her hesitation. She knew how much she felt for him, but they had not even kissed each other. Their relationship had been based on their friendship, deep thinking, and agreement in concepts and values—all of which was accompanied by a hidden attraction. But nothing had happened between them. Trying at that moment was too dangerous; it would have meant cheating on her boyfriend before the wedding. If there had been a chance to consider this, destiny would show them it was meant to be that way, because a month later something happened that would prevent Clara from taking that chance.

Daniel arrived at Clara's house and she told him that she had read the letter and found a few mistakes that were surely imperceptible in relation to the content of what he had written. He anxiously waited for her comments, a reply.

"Why now? Why not before?" Clara asked.

"Perhaps, as it says in the letter, because I was afraid," he answered.

"Yes ... if you had only given me this letter two or three years ago ..." she said in a mixture of pain and anger due to the powerlessness of not being able to make such a decision. "How could I leave my boyfriend now, once I have been supporting him after his little sister's road accident? It would be so cruel to do this to him at this moment before the wedding."

Daniel was shocked by her reply. Deep inside his soul he knew that if she had said *No, Daniel. I only feel a deep friendship for you. Thank you but my reply is no. I cannot leave everything and go with you* ...if it had been so, he would have left Clara's house that day, obliged to forget an unrequited love.

But it had not been so! She was, in some way, saying *yes*. She was saying *she couldn't make such a decision*, not *she didn't want to go with him*.

Clara could neither reply *no* nor *yes* to his proposal. She was shocked; she didn't expect him to confess his feelings so plainly just at that moment. Deep inside she thought she had a special feeling toward him, but up until then she could not tell whether or not he loved her. That same day she suggested they stop their lessons in order not to hurt each other.

That would be their last lesson and the beginning of their separated lives. That would be the last day Clara saw Daniel for a very long time.

Clara found the strength, courage, and sense of sacrifice to accompany Daniel to the door. She led him to the garden exit from where he usually left with his motorbike, not to the hall at the front door.

He felt hurt. She wanted to avoid the possibility of an intimate kiss, although she desired it. She was trying to hide the reason she didn't want him to come close to her. Clara was absolutely certain that if Daniel managed to steal a kiss from her, she would leave everything behind.

A month later, Clara was devastated by the death of her grandmother. If at any point she was considering Daniel's proposal, this event did not help her modify anything. She was worried not only about her boyfriend's reaction but also by what her mother would feel if she broke everything then—just two months before the wedding—to escape to another country just when her mother's mother had died. Clara thought it wouldn't be good to do this to her mother or to her boyfriend.

Clara's adorable Nonna had left Europe during the war, just like thousands of other immigrants overwhelmed by the pain and horrors of death and despair. These were the same immigrants who had arrived at this *blessed land*, as she would say—a country that had opened its doors and welcomed them. Nonna had been born poor in a small town called Enego, situated at the top of a mountain in northern Italy. She was the last one of nine children. Her mother was a widow whom she painfully never saw again after fleeing to Argentina.

Nonna was an unconventional grandmother who could adapt herself to young people's conversations as well as to those of the middle aged and elderly. Everybody loved her. Clara visited her very often. She used to go to her house to take care of her, staying during the night so as not to leave her granny alone. Clara recalled her silent complicity when Daniel called her on the phone. In those days, not everybody had a telephone at home in Argentina. Clara did not have one at her parents' house. But Nonna did have one. So, when Clara spent the night there, Daniel phoned her. And, as usual, they spent one or two hours talking on the phone. Her granny would silently drink *mate* while they talked, or she would leave the kitchen (where the telephone was) in order to respect the link she perceived between them in their conversations.

Daniel found out that Nonna had passed away and decided to go to the wake to see his friend Clara. When he arrived at the corner of the street, he saw her surrounded by her family and boyfriend. He was deeply hurt to see her so close to another man. The pain he felt at that moment impeded him from going up to her.

He stood at the corner of Villate and Maipú next to the presidential residence in Olivos in front of where the wake was taking place and observed her without her ever noticing.

That was the last time Daniel saw Clara before leaving.

But Clara didn't know he was there. She didn't know he was standing at that corner.

Even through the pain of losing her grandmother, the wedding, and honeymoon arrangements, Clara never stopped thinking about Daniel. It was hard for her to overcome the fact that he had been hiding his love for her the same way she had been. On the one hand, she loved her boyfriend—or at least she believed so. She had always respected him. But she knew Daniel was someone special in her life. Clara was a woman who had clear ideas and respected herself as well as others. As any human being experiences, her feelings went from loyalty to hesitation, from respectfulness to temptation, from certainty to doubt. A mixture of emotions invaded her body and mind.

A month and a half later, the day of her wedding was fast approaching. Clara got married, and very deep down that day, she had a feeling that Daniel could show up at the church. She imagined—and even had a vision of—Daniel coming to look for her, like in the movies, to stop the marriage. Maybe it was not conscious, but that was what she would have wanted to happen. Finally, she left on her honeymoon to Polynesia without hearing from Daniel again.

Chapter 2

Northern Hemisphere: Stockholm

- Space: Stockholm, Sweden, Europe.
- Time: March 1988. Seven days before Clara's wedding.

George was smoking while he paced at the airport. Arlanda is a comfortable airport that offers suitable places to rest or work during your wait. It is said that the music of ABBA sounds down the corridors, welcoming foreigners as they come to this beautiful land.

George had been waiting a long time for the arrival of the flight from Argentina that would bring his younger brother to this land. Seven days before Clara's wedding, Daniel was on his flight to Sweden, and he could not stop thinking about what had happened. Hurt and resigned, he remembered when he had given Clara the letter. He had just found out that he was traveling to Sweden. Daniel thought: *I have to learn English. Clara—my friend, my impossible love, my goddess, the woman I have desired the most in my life.*

He had heard from a friend of his that she was about to get married.

Daniel kept on thinking, *I hope she will be happy. I believed at that moment, that I could only give her my love and pamper her. But at twenty -three I already knew that apart from that, you had to have a job, a house, and material things that I could not offer her.*

He continued his thinking with a decision. *I am going to see her and try to take some more English lessons. Deep down I wanted to see her and spend some time with her before leaving Argentina. I had told my friends I was leaving for a year, but I felt it was going to be for a longer time. I had to see her again before leaving the country—and confess my feelings for her! I felt she had to know, although it was too late. My impossible love was on the way to the aisle.*

Daniel continued recalling some precious moments. *One afternoon I got into the car and decided to see her. I was nervous. I did not know how she was going to react or if she could help me. I parked not far away from her house. While walking toward her house, I felt and remembered many moments and conversations we shared when I was in my teens. We had a very special communication and deep dialogues. My heart was pounding faster than usual. Maybe I did not realize how much I loved Clara.*

I rang the doorbell. Clara came out … a smile, a special look in her eyes. I noticed how happy she was to see me after we hadn't heard from each other for such a long time. She let me in immediately. I realized I was still in love with her. She offered me her help and we started with the English lessons. Our conversations became deeper and deeper.

I had the feeling that my trip was something I had to do, but I also felt that the woman of my life had already crossed my path, and—because I was a fool and a coward—I hadn't dared to tell her before. I would never meet anybody like her. But life went on. She was getting married.

And he wondered, *would she do what they do in the movies and leave the groom at the altar?*

I gave her a book called Living, Loving and Learning *by Leo Buscaglia. I remember she liked it, and we used to talk a lot about the book during our English lessons. I noticed she looked very beautiful when we met, as she always did. When I looked straight into her eyes, mm! How amazing! My heart started pounding.*

I decided to write a letter in which I would describe my feelings—but it had to be in English. It was quite hard for me, but I did it. My English was not so good, but I thought that as she was an English teacher, I wanted it to be something special.

In this way, immersed in his thoughts, Daniel crossed the sky on his way to his destination over ten thousand miles from Buenos Aires. It was a long trip, but time seemed like nothing compared to the distance. And it would change into a magic trick, capable of making part of a life disappear in an instant.

Stockholm was a unique city, one of the most beautiful in the world. It had a special touch of magic. Daniel looked through the plane window. He could see yachts and some sailing boats along the coast. The water was still frozen on the archipelago that flowed into the Baltic Sea.

The Royal Palace and the Houses of Parliament could be seen rising imposingly under a sky painted with blue, grey, and fuchsia strokes in the Nordic twilight. Daniel felt immersed in the cultural diversity that surrounded him. He observed each place he loved and was enchanted by such beauty. Perhaps this extremely beautiful and faraway land would be a balm for the pain in his heart.

He thought, *maybe being so far away from Clara will make it easier to forget her.*

He allowed himself to be carried away by the majestic, captivating scenery, but he could not figure out how he would forget her. When he wrote that letter, he had promised he never would.

Now, without realizing it, he would be trapped in the forces of karma that would take him along centuries through history—until he could act on his love for Clara if fate ever reunited them.

Suddenly his brother interrupted his thoughts.

"Hey, dude, where are you? Do you like it? Isn't it gorgeous?" asked George.

"Yes, it is beautiful!" Daniel answered.

"I would say you are impressed or ... I don't know, it seems as if you were not here. You are *here*, you know that? You are no longer in Argentina!" his brother said enthusiastically.

"Yes, I know. Everything is all right. I am very happy to be with you," added Daniel.

They hugged each other, and George tapped Daniel on his back to show him that he was also happy to have him there. They had a coffee together in a pub before they headed for George's flat and reminisced about old times they had shared some years before in Mendoza, in the Andes in Argentina. The pub was in the basement of a sixteenth-century building. It had a low roof and a façade decorated in ancient bricks.

While they were having coffee, Daniel wanted to know more about the city. George briefly told him that nearby, in Djurgarden Island, there was the Vasa Museum, in which people could see the remains of the world's most ancient warship that had sunk in 1628 and had been rescued from the riverbed 330 years later. Daniel looked at a poster on the wall. The green lawns and captivating meadows formed mostly by farms showed the scenery splashed by carmine when you observed the small red painted cabins. This landscape, was one of the aspects of the Swedish culture he got to learn from that moment on. Its only view made him feel bathed in the Nordic folklore every step of his way.

As they went to the street again, Daniel was amazed by what he saw: a group of people standing on a corner waiting for the traffic light to switch colors so they could cross. All of them were looking up to the sky. He couldn't come out of his shock, since on the following block the same event was taking place. Suddenly, he asked his brother what those people were doing. George told him that they were using that moment to tan. Amazing! Considering Argentina's blazing sunshine, he would never have thought of witnessing something like that. Anyway, there would come a time when he, Swedish style, would be part of a similar scene.

As Daniel started to settle down in the place, he saw for himself the beauty of this land of Nobel prizes, scientific and technological advances, designers and wood craftsmen—just some of the many virtues that characterized the Swedish.

From that moment on, Daniel started his life on the other side of the world, waiting to see what destiny—which is nothing other than one's decisions—had in store for him. It is about the choices we make. It's as if two paths are presented to us, and we have to decide which one to take.

According to the chosen path, certain things will happen in that person's life. There is something that simply cannot be explained, something that seems to somehow bend that road in search of an alternative one—which seems to be the one we didn't choose at that moment.

If the road is the right one, it will find you one way or another at some moment. Maybe it happens in times that aren't easy to understand, but once we've accomplished what we had to do, they become that possibility we yearn for.

It was seven days before Clara's wedding when Daniel left for Sweden. From the moment he stepped on Swedish land, Daniel learned about life far away from his own land about the effort needed to learn a complicated, somehow weird language. He learned about adapting to a different society, about comfort, order, technology ... and *cold*.

As soon as he got to Sweden, Daniel realized how different Swedish culture was from his own country's culture. Sweden's geographical position in the world influenced its culture and customs—the way people dressed, what they ate, and many other aspects. Being so close to the North Pole was something Daniel had not experienced before. From the cold he learned to appreciate the snowflakes painting the beautiful setting. From the cold he learned to value a single ray of sun that appeared in the morning. He learned to value a single ray of light and clarity as spring came closer.

Being forced to learn a foreign language had put him in a pickle more than once. Fortunately many of these occasions seemed to be funny. Sometimes he mispronounced a vowel, turning a word that he had so effortlessly pronounced with conviction into a bad word or insult. More than once he found himself being the object of laughter, and sometimes a misunderstanding had to be explained afterward, when somebody else told him what had happened.

He learned that when Swedes get mad, they do not shout. They never raised their voices like people did in Argentina.

Daniel also learned from the moment he arrived in Sweden that Swedish vowels are longer; the sound spreads a bit when you talk. This was something Daniel had a hard time with when implementing it in his speech. It may have been what gave him that foreign accent among those fair-haired Vikings.

After many years, Daniel grew to understand that when a Swede gets mad with someone, he shows his anger by shortening the vowels—not by shouting. Words become shorter and sound a little dry. Since Daniel hadn't been able to modify this part of his pronunciation of the language, many times through the years he found himself in front of somebody who asked him if he was angry. When this happened, he had to answer *no* and explain—in *Swedish* no less!

The first years were really tough, struggling and adapting, working endless hours and taking what work he could get without knowing the language. He found himself working in office buildings, washing dishes at restaurants, and delivering butter and milk in a van at 4 a.m. in the winter. Swedish winters average temperatures between twenty degrees below zero—even thirty or forty below.

Daniel also had to adapt to certain customs that were very different from those in South America. For example, when talking to somebody, you always have to keep a distance of one and a half meters. People say *hello* and shake hands once; if you bump into that person at another time of the day, don't even think of shaking hands again. You've already seen each other and said *hi*.

This is completely strange for us in Argentina, since we tend to hug and kiss. Why not shake hands for no reason at all every time we bump into a friend?

In Sweden, if you are thinking of sharing a coffee with somebody, you cannot go to his or her house just *because*. You have to arrange a visit in the next couple of weeks to his or your house. You also can't call somebody on the phone without thinking that you may be interrupting them. This is actually seen as impolite or rude. Daniel started to adjust himself to the habits of a culture that was simply different from Argentina´s.

Unlike in Sweden, it's very typical in Argentina to show up at friends' houses without warning. It's also very likely that you will be invited in for a spontaneous barbecue or to order a spur-of-the-moment pizza to share. This attitude is not seen as rude. In any case, if the owners of the house can't have friends over at that time, they will tell you and rearrange a visit.

Daniel finally adapted to the culture, and with time he managed to progress. He enjoyed some years of traveling around Europe. He went all over Germany, Holland, France, and Switzerland. In Switzerland he searched for stories about his ancestors, especially about Sion, the town in which his grandfather had been. It was surprising to think that Clara's grandparents had been born in northern Italy—right next to Switzerland, where Daniel's grandparents lived.

Now he was in Sweden and Clara was in Argentina.

Chapter 3

Southern Hemisphere: Buenos Aires

Both Clara and Daniel had been born In Buenos Aires, located on the banks of Rio de la Plata. It is said that when Pedro de Mendoza disembarked his Spanish ship in the sixteenth century, he was shocked by the purity of the air he was breathing. This first impression of his is what led to our city's name. Nowadays Buenos Aires is a huge urban center similar to many advanced cities.

However, Buenos Aires hasn't lost its impeccable and magical light blue sky or its fresh air, because it is at the banks of a huge river that flows into the Atlantic Ocean. The whole east coast of Argentina has its boundaries by this vast ocean. The coast covers the typical summer resort city of Mar del Plata, past Peninsula de Valdez to the south with its penguin colonies and killer whales—to Ushuaia, the most southern city in the world in Tierra del Fuego (Land of Fire), up to the Argentinian Antarctica. Antarctica—the ice desert that motivates the bravest scientists and researchers— represents a most desired object for the powerful. It is the coveted natural resource of fresh, clean water.

Clara loved her city. Buenos Aires resembles Paris, something that surprises many tourists from around the world who think they are at the end of the world. On the contrary, they find a welcoming city ready to be enjoyed during both day and night at any time of the year. Its buildings are mostly built in French architectural style and they are splashed along 9 de Julio Avenue, the widest avenue in the world. Two big boulevards are covered with old jacaranda and palo borracho treetops that spread a soft violet and pink florescence during springtime.

Each day Clara observed the sky from the streets in her neighborhood. A similar color was not easily seen in Sweden. It was the purest light blue sky anyone could imagine.

- Place: Buenos Aires, Argentina.
- Time: 2001, 13 years later.

Clara was at university having a leadership strategy lesson. The subject was very interesting, but her mind was a bit busy with the conflicts she was confronting at the moment. At last, after a long time of constant disagreement, she had made the hard decision to divorce her husband. That morning her husband had left home. She felt that the only thing their children were going to learn if they stayed together was a misconception of what love was. She felt they would think that living together meant quarrelling and disagreeing, trying not to see each other, or escaping from one another even—even while living under the same roof. And love is not that.

She left the class and had a coffee with a classmate named Stella. Since Stella had already been through a divorce, Clara hoped she could offer some insight.

"Hey, Stella!" said Clara.

"Yes," she answered.

"I must tell you something," said Clara.

"What are you going to tell me? You found a lover?" Stella asked, smiling.

"No …not at all … my husband left this morning," declared Clara.

"*Really?*" exclaimed Stella, astonished. "Well, according to what you have been telling me, it is going to be the best choice."

"Yes, sure," said Clara. "But now starts the battle. He's like *crazy*. This is not going to be easy for me."

"It is never going to be worse than going through the torture of living every day of your life with somebody who was not meant for you. This means to suffer daily; it keeps on destroying you little by little. It is bad for both of you and of course for the children," answered Stella in a calm, confident way.

Clara nodded in agreement and they continued talking during break time while having a coffee. Suddenly Stella asked her:

"Tell me ... and *you*? Did you have a boyfriend before meeting your husband, someone who you had fallen in love with?"

Clara did not clearly understand why she was asking her this question at that moment. Her mind was busy with what was going on. But she found herself suddenly answering the question spontaneously.

"Well, he was not my boyfriend. We were just friends," replied Clara. "But if I have to say I was in love with somebody, that person was Daniel," she added.

The next thing she knew, Clara had jumped back in time and was telling Stella who Daniel was.

"Daniel was a friend of one of my best friend's brothers. I met him at Anna's house, my friend. We saw each other there in different meetings and we made friends easily due to our long conversations and natural agreement.

One day, he asked me if I could help him with English because he was running the risk of losing his vacancy. His father had just died and I accepted helping him at once. He came home every Friday and Saturday because he was enrolled in a boarding school. Sometimes he came on a Sunday.

He was only sixteen, however I felt deeply attracted by his thoughts. In the role of a teacher my attitude was always focused on teaching him as well as possible to help him pass the exam, especially during this hard time he was going through.

- Place: Buenos Aires.
- Time: 2005, four years later.

Clara's living room was a cozy and welcoming place where she and Stella would work together on university projects. That day, when she went upstairs to look for some information Stella had asked her for, Clara ended up sobbing while reading Daniel's letter. The whole letter reminded her of how deep his words had been. As she read it again and again, she started discovering many things she hadn't realized when he had first given it to her. The full letter read:

This story is my story of impossible love. She is the most beautiful woman in the world. I have always liked her. When I saw her for the first time my heart started beating. I have always loved her, for years. But I did not tell her because I was afraid. I dream of her. She hugs me in her arms and tenderly kisses me. In the sky among the stars. She is my life. Can I have your love today or tomorrow? When I have it I will be really happy. You are an excellent human being. I will never find someone like you. I LOVE YOU. If this feeling is inside me I will never let it go. It is something I need. It is difficult to explain. It is you, the one I have been looking for day by day. Well, I don't know what you think. Now I am leaving for Europe, and I don't know when I am coming back. I need to tell you before leaving.

I will remember you and love you ALWAYS.

If you love me, will you come with me.

Stella listened to her as she started reading, but she ended up snatching the paper out of her hands, since Clara was overcome with profound emotions that filled her soul and she could not continue reading.

"Hey girl, this guy really loves you!" exclaimed Stella.

"Well, that was long ago," said Clara, feeling somewhat sad.

"Well, and you are not far from being in love! Otherwise, tell me—why would you be crying this way?" added Stella.

"It is true. I am surprised by the way I feel and also by how I reacted as soon as I started reading the letter," confessed Clara to her friend.

"It is evident that you have kept this feeling inside for a very long time. Look! I am going to tell you something and I want you to listen to me carefully. I do not want to come to study here next Saturday and find out that you haven't done anything to get his email address. Clear?" pointed out Stella.

Clara listened to her attentively. But from that moment on she did not need more encouragement. She started feeling an unexplainable strength, something she could not properly describe but that was leading her to her objective.

This perception was something she had never felt before. It was as if someone or some external force were pushing her to find out and not letting her stop. She could feel that impulse. How could she explain it? It was as if someone were pushing her, but not because she did not want to. It did not have to do with the desire. It was just that *something* was pushing her forward.

This way, after trying to contact Fabian, a friend of Daniel's who had gone to school with him in Argentina, Clara could get Daniel's email. In the beginning it was not easy; Fabian felt jealous because Clara wanted to contact Daniel after so much time. But after two or three days, Fabian sent Daniel's e-mail to her.

Now she had to dare to write to him and wait for an answer—if he had the intention of answering.

Clara was doubtful. She thought that perhaps he would say, "Now, this girl is writing to me after seventeen years of not having exchanged even one word?"

On the other hand she felt she had to tell him what had happened. She felt she had to, at least for him to feel loved, to feel good about it. She had to confess her feelings toward him.

- Space: Buenos Aires
- Time: March 2005

It was a hot, wet, summer day in Buenos Aires. Clara regained courage and wrote a letter. Her first e-mail:

To: daniel@lovemail.com
From: clara@lovemail.com
Subject: AFTER SUCH A LONG TIME

Hello Daniel,

How are you?

I guess you must be really surprised to receive this e-mail.

I was really doubting whether to write or not but it seems I finally dared to do it. Actually, I am going through a period of time in my life that is rich in any aspect related to finding my inner self. I feel connected to personal growing, professionally and as a human being.

Along this search I find parts of my life on the way which I analyze sometimes with emotion, some other times with pain and with hope as well. I'm determined to rebuild those kinds of relationships that had a deep meaning and were important to me. Or either would have had a quality not easy to be found. And I found myself, thinking, once again ... about you.

Besides, as things you love and value most, are taken care for ... or you cannot throw them away. I found the letters you sent me from Mendoza, and the last one you left before leaving to Europe. You and I had a bond that I still value most. I would like this to be a time for healing the soul and the souls that could have been affected by mine.

I would like to know about you, what you did during all these years, hoping to find you full of life as I feel I remember you the last time I saw you. It is said that people are, as they grow, mostly "more of the same." So I am certain I will find you richer inside than you were in those times. And for sure, you must have surpassed me in many aspects … And most probably, you speak English better than I do.

Life sometimes turns things upside down and the one who was teaching before might be now learning from the apprentice … no?

Anyway I have always learned more from you than what I taught you. I hope you are willing to answer to the huge impulse that pushed me to contact you.

Big kiss,
Clara.
♥

Now she had to wait. Perhaps he would answer, or perhaps he'd only be polite and not want to connect with her after such a long time.

Perhaps he wouldn't even receive the e-mail or it would get lost. Who knew what would happen? Clara anxiously waited until the following day, hoping that he had been able to read her mail.

Immersed in his routine, in his living room at home in Stockholm, Daniel was getting ready to check his e-mail box.

It was snowing outside. Snowflakes fell slowly over the treetops painting them in an impeccable white, somewhat transparent color. The ice seemed to sharply cut the green leaves which were hidden from view.

Sitting in front of the computer, Daniel started looking at the list of new messages. He had just woken up. His eyes tried to close again even though he had washed them a few minutes before in the bathroom. He rubbed his eyes while he yawned.

Suddenly, among all the Swedish names that headed the e-mails, he read something in Spanish: *Clara.*

No! He couldn't believe it. At the beginning, it was like a dream. He didn't understand what he was reading. He almost deleted the e-mail, thinking it could be a computer virus. He read it again.

He was overtaken by emotion so deeply that he could almost perceive his body quivering. So he turned off the computer and he went to the kitchen.

He could not believe it! Reading Clara's name after such a long time made him recall the communication he had had with her so long ago. He was deeply moved and he also felt it could not be possible. He waited for a short moment. It was as if he needed to take some time to believe that what he was looking at was possible-—that it was real. He felt overwhelmed with happiness and totally surprised. *Seventeen years* had passed since he had last seen Clara or even talked to her.

Once in the kitchen, Daniel prepared some coffee and went back to the computer, certain that nothing had happened. He was sure he had simply had a dream—that he had just gotten up and the day had just begun.

Everything started again.

This time, he was holding a smoky cup of coffee emanating a delicious smell that filled the room, but his sense of smell seemed to be blocked.

He went back to the computer as he swallowed the coffee that had no taste at all. It was not because coffee in Sweden was disgusting, no. It was because he did it on auto pilot; the liquid flowed down his throat forgetting to leave signs on his taste buds. The coffee had no taste due to his strong emotion, the expectation underlying his acts.

The *beep* of the computer turning on and the sparkling light on the screen as it restarted seemed to him a slow, black and white motion picture, endless and eternal.

Daniel wrote his name and password as fast as he could. He waited. The e-mail opened up. Clara's name and surname appeared on the message title. The subject line was in English.

It was true! Clara was there. He opened it. He read it almost without believing his eyes. Daniel answered:

To: clara@lovemail.com
From: daniel@lovemail.com
Subject: Reply to AFTER SUCH A LONG TIME

Hellooo!

It's so moving! I can't believe it! It's you! While I was reading your email I felt a deep emotion, difficult to explain. I was completely moved. It's so good to know that you followed your impulse and wrote to me. I was about to do it several times but, if it is worthwhile knowing, I never forgot you. I have really good memories and you are in my list—needless to say it is very short—of very special people. Whenever I was feeling down I took you out of the little box where I keep the beautiful things about life and remembered you and that helped me to forget the bad times.

Whenever I contacted Fabian, I asked him if he knew something about you. The last time I talked to him, he told me he had met you and that you have talked about me ... And I told him "Does she still remember me?" Where should I start, my English is not very good, I only speak Swedish. I understand English but when I want to say something it only comes out in Swedish. I should have taken more lessons with you, the most beautiful teacher. This is all so crazy! Writing to you after such a long time, six days before you got married I left Argentina. It's now seventeen years since I left and I never went back.

Every year I plan going, but due to any other reason I spend my holidays in Europe. In any case, if I go to Buenos Aires sometime, I plan to visit you and ... imagine how I am going to hug you! Well now, telling you a bit about these years, about my life here in Sweden—which will soon almost be the same amount I lived in Buenos Aires—I got married as soon as I arrived. I met a girl and in a month we were married. My children ...

Clara stopped reading and many thoughts came to her mind.

Daniel had answered Clara's e-mail the day after she had sent the letter. He had been totally moved and surprised by what life was putting in front of his eyes and through the computer screen. Once again, time and space converged—this time through the computer screen. This shortened the distance that destiny had marked in their lives.

Clara continued reading Daniel's letter:

...I got married as soon as I arrived.

Clara thought that he might have done it in a hurry, just because he needed to stay there, or perhaps because she had gotten married and so he did the same.

She kept on reading:

... I have been working like a dog from the very first day I came to this country. I only had 200 dollars when I arrived. I worked washing dishes in restaurants, cleaning offices and after a year and a half when I had already learnt some words in Swedish I started a new job and learnt the language at work "Der var inte latt at lara sig svenska" "It´s not easy to learn Swedish." I could go forward with great effort but I had some bad luck, as I got ill long ago, and next week I am going to be operated on.

Well, let's see if you tell me something about your life, do you have children, house, fiancé? Where do you live? Do you have a telephone number where I can call you? I hope you keep on writing and not losing contact with you. Do you know of any chat where we can meet? Think that here we are five hours forward than in Argentina.

A Kiss,
Daniel
♥

Daniel finished writing his answer to Clara and immediately he connected again and wrote a second email:

To: clara@lovemail.com
From: daniel@lovemail.com
Subject: Hello again!

Hi Clara! I read your letter one more time and I felt deeply moved once again. And now I realize what I feel when I read it for the second time or third time. I felt the same way I felt when I received your letters while I was living in Mendoza. I kept your letters in any pocket and I read them once and again until I knew them by heart, such good memories! I have never met someone as special as you, I just wanted to tell you this.

Daniel.

♥

It was incredible. Daniel had answered her e-mail feeling the same emotion she had felt, and he was repeating the words he had written seventeen years before in the letter he gave her: *I will never meet someone like you.* Or when he wrote *I will never forget you.* It was the same phrase he had written in that letter he had given her before her wedding. He was using almost the same expression. Daniel phrased it this time as *I never forgot you.*

Coincidentally, as with events like this that are hard to believe, Clara had kept Daniel's original letter for such a long time in a little box. And he had written—in his first e-mail after seventeen years—that *he had a little box where he kept the beautiful things of life!*

Their connection was not forgotten. Clara got to know that everything was exactly the same, as though time had not passed by and the distance between them had not existed. As if the Atlantic Ocean had a bridge that was only eight yards long, instead of there being over ten thousand miles between them.

The power of love makes any distance incapable of separating what should be united; some things remains together in spite of space and time. It's a kind of love so powerful and strong that it seems to have existed, untouched inside their souls and hearts, all along for centuries.

Clara read Daniel's answer and immediately wrote:

To: daniel@lovemail.com
From: clara@lovemail.com
Subject: I CAN HARDLY BELIEVE IT

Hi Daniel,

It's so lucky that my email did not get lost! Reading your email was truly moving to me. Can you imagine me sitting in front of the computer, feeling the emotion going down through my throat and tears rolling down on my cheeks? ... Reading and re-reading each of your words?

Tell me, did you really ask Fabian if I remembered you? I could never forget you. It took several years not to remember your birthday that day, and some other things I will tell you further on. I have a telephone number, but for the time being I am not going to give it to you as it would be really hard to handle the emotion if I could hear your voice right now. Let us take some time writing first, ok?

Now let me tell you, I got married on the date it was planned. When I read your letter I realized that it was just a few days after you left. My beautiful children have grown a lot. We bought a house, moved and then I made the decision of separating almost four years ago.

I continue teaching and made a second career at the same time I dealt with the house, the job, the children, the divorce, the lawyer, the judges, the trial … well I am not going to bother you talking about sad things.

I work a lot for me and my children. You know? When I divorced many people told me "now you must catch a man full of money" fool of them … they don't know that the most important thing in life is LOVE and when you find it you do not have to let it go, you must take care of it; how much money somebody has is not important, you are not happy due to money, money does not fill the deep cavities of the soul, neither does it make you link your body with your couple.

Boyfriends? There was a pair, nothing important. A bit surprised because most men of thirtysomething follow me and at forty two I find it surprising!

I am deeply worried as you told me you are ill. The day of the operation, that's to say, next week, you can count on me, I will be thinking about you all day long. Everything is gonna be all right! Neither have I ever met someone like you, I just wanted you to know.

Take care,
Clara.
♥

The following day Clara received a new email.

To: clara@lovemail.com
From: daniel@lovemail.com
Subject: Reply to I CAN HARDLY BELIEVE IT

Hi!

It's so crazy! After such a long time and feeling so much emotion! I am anxiously waiting for your telephone number. Congratulations on your career and because you keep on doing what you like most. Doing what one likes has helped me a lot to survive in this country.

This is a totally different society than ours, but after such a long time, one gets used to it and starts forgetting some things, but never the people you love, who you never forget. This matter about the distance is quite hard ... you think a lot about what you left or how it would have been if one had decided to stay or gone back. One will never know that, it is something you think or dream of. But the positive aspect about it is that you have good memories and that you can recall them to be able to go through bad moments here.

When I got ill, two years ago, I got depressed. But looking at the positive side of things I realized many things you cannot see when you are busy at work and solving problems. And you, beauty? How do you feel? The guys of about thirty something is not surprising to me, you are the most beautiful woman in Argentina. You cannot imagine how much I would like to see you!

Do you know what I remember? When I was living in Mendoza I once went to visit you and we went out one night to have a coffee around La Lucila, we had been talking a lot and you were so stunning. I looked at the other men watching you, I felt like Maradona, sitting in a café with such a stunning woman. When we were walking to the car, you told me you were feeling cold, so I gave you my jacket or pullover. It was so stupid of me! I should have hugged you and not ever let go. Maybe thanks to my being so stupid we are now writing to each other after so many years. I was feeling afraid because I thought that such a goddess deserved a man full of money, a man that could give her all she wanted and I felt I could not give you this kind of pleasures-—regarding the economic aspect—because on another level I could have given you whatever you wanted.

Well goddess, I hope you write back to me and you give me your telephone number. This reminds me about the times when

I was young and met somebody and the most important thing was if you could get the telephone number, which was not easy.

Hugs,
Daniel

To: daniel@lovemail.com
From: clara@lovemail.com
Subject: In spite of the distance.

Hi Daniel,

How are you?

Thinking about all this I remember your words "It's so crazy" after such a long time ... Can someone be so close to somebody else in spite of the distance? I think this has always happened to us. It has always been very strong the bond that united us, do you feel the same? At least this is how I feel it.

I don't know how it happened but as I was looking for something else— I was checking a little box—when I suddenly found the letter you gave me before leaving. I started reading it and couldn't finish reading it clearly because a deep emotion invaded my body and soul. After some days I called Fabian and asked him for your email. He said: "Hey look, take into account that you were Daniel's impossible love." I replied: "Ah really?" What I did not tell him was: "And he was mine." Why should I tell him, no? If there was someone I would tell, it would be you. I hope that reading this makes you feel well, this way I give you what I could never give you, at least in words.

Of course I remember when we went to La Lucila to have some coffee together. And when we were coming back we were listening to a Barbara Streisand song. I don't remember the name, do you?

I was a goddess, don't you forget I was twenty two or twenty three years younger. Now I am twenty years older. It sounds horrible! Ha ... ha. I still keep some resemblance to a goddess. Well, if I was a goddess, you were the owner of Mount Olympus, you had your goddess there, and she was with you, not with the ones watching. But you didn't dare to, the same that happened to me when you gave me the letter only three months before my wedding asking me to go with you to Europe. I had the party, the furniture, the dress, everything ready. Yes, it was strong and hard. I couldn't leave my ex-husband after the tragedy he had gone through. It implied making a decision in a very short span of time. If only had you told me that before, if I had had more time!

Life can take many twists and turns. Now it's hard to think I could not be happy with him and I let you go. You know? That day when we were at my parent's house and you were leaving, I let you leave the house through the garden gate, because it was more exposed. And I did not choose to use the living room hall for you to leave because I was terrified of what you could do—not because of a kiss of course—but because I knew, I was certain that if I tried your mouth's taste I would have had to leave everything behind.

I was a fool! But, as you said, perhaps we wouldn't be writing to each other right now. I am sure that if the communication between us still remains the way it has always been, on another level, of course you would have been able to give me whatever I wanted, and I would have answered the same way.

Well god, write to me, take care, rest and get over, I want you to put into your mind a special thought: You are getting better right now! Yes or yes. Are you listening to me? Do you understand? You are already better.

Sending you a kiss.
Clara.

♥

To: clara@lovemail.com
From: daniel@lovemail.com
Subject: Hi Goddess!

I am feeling better and I can't stop thinking of you, not even for a moment. Of course I feel the same as you, all what you wrote about space and time and our friends relationship? … or eternal lovers, in love with our personalities, in love with the way in which we communicate. It has always been very special the way I communicated with you. I could always be myself, I don't know if you understand me. I felt, whenever I met you or talked to you and looked into your eyes, I felt I could be inside you, It was as if, through your eyes, I could see … or better say … you let me see you till your heart. And I felt so well when I shared time with you, an English lesson, just a visit. I just settled for looking at you.

Well I am a bit melancholic. Let me tell you that the operation went on well. It hurts but the medicine for pain is having effect although it makes me feel dizzy, I just wanted to write some lines to let you know that I am ok.

Take care beauty,
Daniel.
♥

Clara replied and told him something that was going to leave them both astonished.

To: daniel@lovemail.com
From: clara@lovemail.com
Subject: Remember that song?

Hi Daniel,

What lovely things you wrote about the look! I also feel I can be myself when I am with you. With you I can be so natural.

Nobody knows me as you do. You get it? They can praise me with the most seductive phrases but, to me, they are only anecdotic, they do not mean anything else but a satisfaction to my ego—only you can get so deep in me. You were my teacher.

Life means constantly learning and if one does not learn from what happens to ourselves in life … one loses life, don't you think so? Even what makes you suffer teaches you something, and from these experiences one learns, if it is possible, to be a better person. On my night table I have the book you gave me as a present, written by Leo Buscaglia "Living, Loving and Learning," I am re reading it once again, then I will send you some phrases to share. Thank you for giving it to me.

I want to tell you how I got to write to you. I once again feel astonished by all this! I think: "What was it that made me read the letter when I found it?" The emotion I felt does not surprise me, it is evident that it has to do with the feelings. What shocks me is that it was as if something pushed me to do it. It's so difficult to explain, I believe it is not easy to be understood if you have not gone through it.

May I tell you something else? Yesterday I was listening to the radio and they were playing the song you played in the car that night we went out for a coffee in La Lucila. Remember you made me translate it for you to understand it? Well, I stood on the kitchen floor next to the radio listening to it and I listened: "I am a woman in love and I'll do anything to get you into my world and hold you within." And the song goes on. But there's a part that seemed sort of premonitory to me.

"We may be oceans away, in love there is no measure of time." I don´t know if it was in that sequence. But listening to the phrase: "We may be oceans away!" "In love there's no measure of time!" It is unbelievable! You chose that song almost 6 years before leaving to Europe and at that time you hadn't the slightest idea that one day you were going to live in Europe. And I am just now realizing the content of the lyrics of the song … I cannot be more amazed! This is unbelievable! I want you to know that

I did not get up one morning and say: What about Daniel's life? I am going to write to him to see what happens … No! I could only say that it was as if someone from heaven had shaken me, pushed me forward … I was suffused by a force beyond me … that pushed me to look for you.

I leave you with this.

I think of you.

Write to me when you can, when you feel well, now take a rest. I wait for you.

Clara.

♥

Premonitions, marked destiny, causality? What is it that takes place in a magical way and we sometimes cannot see it? What don't we allow ourselves to listen to? What the heart tells us. Why do we remain deaf to many things in life?

Why had Daniel chosen that song at that moment? Why did he write the exact words on that copybook paper? What kind of force led him to choose a song with the lyrics *we may be oceans apart* without knowing that destiny would separate them with the Atlantic Ocean? Or the line *in love there is no measure of time* without knowing they would be separated for seventeen years?

Besides, before leaving, Daniel had written: *Can I have your love today or tomorrow?* How did he know that the possibility of tomorrow was booked in his destiny? He could have written: *Can I have your love today?*

When I say "Why do we remain deaf to many things in life?" I mean everything, not only love. I refer to everything that man ignores or finds easier not to see.

It reminds me of a song that belongs to Phil Collins, "Another Day in Paradise" that retells how a woman who is begging on the streets is ignored by a man who walks past. How many times do we ignore facts or people because we cannot comprehend everything, because we are not interested, because something is not happening to us ... or because we are lucky enough not to be in their shoes?

Who listens to these people? Luckily, there are composers and musicians who, as Collins does, try to help people become aware of these situations through their songs. Luckily, music exists! We have to admit that we are fortunate enough to have great communicators— singers. Beyond fame, would they be aware of what they can achieve in people's lives, of what they are capable of communicating to the world?

We only need to listen ...

We are lucky to have Barbara Streisand and Barry Gibb, Luis Miguel, Mana, Elton John, Gloria Stefan, George Michael, Pavarotti, Zuchero, Sting, ABBA, Roxete, Charles Aznavour, Frank Sinatra, Liza Minelli, Fito Paez, Josiah Barlow, Jairo, Los Nocheros, Los Fabulosos Cadillacs and all of those who I can't mention here because unfortunately the list would be very long.

It's so good to know that Bono uses his fame to help others!

How lucky we are to listen to the lyrics Lennon wrote in "Imagine." His messages have no walls or boundaries—they are understood by all of those who know how to listen to them.

There, where language boundaries are broken.

There, where it does not matter in which language it is said.

There lay the universal messages, those that everybody understands.

Those that can only be transmitted from the soul.

We only need to listen.

Chapter 4

Signs

Clara thinks: *I can hardly believe what Daniel is saying! Seventeen years had passed without talking or seeing each other, without knowing anything about one another, years in which only a phrase coming from someone else was what we knew of one another. And he had never returned back to our country during all that time having not seen his brothers in Argentina, his cousins, or his friends. Now that we started talking again, he is telling me that he'll be here in a month!*

Three months passed after their reunion via e-mail.

Letters started to be more and more personal each time. They both felt that after what they'd been through, they had no inhibitions, misunderstandings, or any other kind of obstacle that could prevent them from showing the love they felt for each other.

He seduced her with words that were filled with love and eroticism, and Clara accepted them, feeling all the love he was offering her. She could accept him right away because their bond over all those years had to do with the fact that they hadn't been separated. Although they really had been separated regarding space, their souls had always been connected through their thinking. He had thought of her every single day of his life on the other side of the world. And she could not forget him. They had been together constantly together in a spiritual way, making their connection unbreakable.

Despite not having seen him in such a long time, Clara could feel something that was difficult to explain. He could make any kind of shyness or discomfort—feelings a woman might have after not seeing someone for so long—go away. She felt he seduced her, but at the same time, he respected her and filled her with love.

They could both sense that they now had to give one another all the love they had been saving. There was nothing stopping them from loving each other. They craved so much for this meeting that life couldn't give them before. Now it was being put in front of them. Now the waters of the Atlantic Ocean were backing down, leaving a flat path that had been long and hard for both of them. Their path had given them moments of joy in their lives, but there had also been plenty of pain, loss, and submission.

"Hello, Clara?" said Mariana.

"Hi, Mariana, my friend. How are you doing?" answered Clara.

"Well, girl. Tell me quickly because I am working right now and I can't talk much. How are things going on with Daniel?"

"Listen to this," Clara answered. "I can't believe it! He is coming!"

"What!?" Mariana said in astonishment, almost shouting.

"Yes!" Clara said. "He is coming here next month. He already has a ticket! I don't want to get my hopes up, but I still can't believe it," replied Clara.

"This is amazing! Great! Have you told anyone else yet?" Mariana asked.

"No, not yet. You are the first one to know. And in fact, I am not going to tell many people. I want to keep it private—only you, your sister, and Stella, of course. Don't forget that she is the one who got me to look for his email address. Amazing, huh? It seems like there are certain times when you meet certain people in a particular place that makes it look as if it has turned out this way for a reason. I feel that what she told me, the whole situation, the way in which I found Daniel's letter when Stella was in my house that day ... hmm ... I don't know. It's as if somebody used her—I could even say an angel that made us closer," explained Clara. "I believe this is a sign," she added.

"What do you mean by a *sign*?" Mariana asked, trying to get Clara's idea.

Clara started to explain it to her:

"What I mean is that Stella was there for a reason. There was something that had to happen at a certain time in Daniel's and my life, and Stella was the means used to send us a message. I understand a sign as something that reaches you if you are open to listen to it. And once you are ready to understand it, it manifests as a message, perhaps written somewhere, that gives you a clue to give meaningful significance to that message. This can also be sent to you through a person that tells you something. If you are ready to listen to it you can find the hidden message," concluded Clara.

"It's amazing. Hard to believe!" murmured Mariana.

"Yes, I can assure you that this is strange, as if it had been written in our destiny so that it had to be this way," added Clara.

"Well, now you have to get ready, buy some new clothes. We can go together if you like! I can't make it this Saturday, but I will be able to the next one, okay?" Mariana said encouragingly.

"Ok, let's do it. I'm incredibly nervous," replied Clara.

"Be cool, girl. This is unbelievable. It's the kind of love story you find in books," said Mariana calmly.

"And am I the star? Is it true or am I dreaming?" Clara wondered aloud.

"It *is* true. And enjoy it, you deserve it. You've been through too much; you have to fully enjoy what is going on now," answered Mariana.

"Yes, my friend. I'll call you later and tell you more about it, okay?" said Clara.

"Okay, we'll talk later, Clara. Bye!"

"Bye, Marianita," said Clara.

Mariana and Clara met in Palermo Hollywood, a one-hundred-year-old neighborhood in Buenos Aires. They strolled together down the old area filled with trees, checking out the clothes. They arrived at a square where multiple streets converged. The place was full of bars and antique stores. In the street, an old man—his face marked with paths of wrinkles that look like avenues—was selling antiques from his broken cart. There was a 1940s doll pram, carved glasses, hand-painted plates with a thin pattern that was drawn precisely, and a heavy siphon of soda made of thick green glass that insisted on lasting over time, stubborn and determined.

The ladies stopped to look around and they started talking to the old man, asking him where he had gotten his antiques. They wanted to know more about him. The old man, who was happy to chat with them, told them a funny story about one of the objects.

Suddenly, some tourists who looked interested in buying some souvenirs, showed up. Clara and Mariana waved the old man goodbye and went to a cafe to talk. From where they were sitting, they could see the square full of people looking at the many street stands, where jewelry was being sold as well as hippy dresses, handmade lamps, shirts, blankets, and scarves. The square was a potpourri of different colors, standing out thanks to the bright afternoon sun on that cool day.

Some minutes later, Mariana's sister Samantha arrived and joined them. Clara was chatting with her friends. They were both artists. Each of them had a style with a certain *something* that showed their love for art in everything they did or said. The three of them enjoyed those moments when they could talk about everything, about what was going on in their lives, but of course they couldn't help talking about Daniel. Samantha, who was very expressive and outgoing, got too excited every time she analyzed the situation.

Mariana gave Clara her unconditional support, and motivated her to enjoy what life sent her way. She was down-to-earth and always kept a realistic perspective on things.

They all got up and went shopping. They entered a very modern store where Clara tried on a dress. While she was in the dressing room changing her clothes, Mariana gave her more clothes that Clara had picked out so she could try them on. The changing room door opened and closed, and the clothes seemed to have movement on their own as they went from her body to the floor, from the seat in the fitting room and back to Clara's body.

Meanwhile, Mariana, who loved everything related to art, made the most of that moment and gave advice to her friend. She also told the saleswoman, in detail, everything about Daniel and Clara's story and how they had found each other again after being separated by seventeen years and over ten thousand miles. She told her about the letter before the wedding and explained that Clara was trying on clothes because Daniel was coming in three weeks! Mariana narrated the story in such a descriptive and exciting way that whoever listened to it felt as if they were living or experiencing it themselves.

The saleswoman said, "But this sounds like a novel!" Mariana answered,

"Yes, it sounds like a novel … but it is actually happening."

Clara tried on several pieces of clothing and decided to take a pair of tight pants, which complimented her body making her look sexy and beautiful.

Daniel and Clara kept on writing to each other. He asked her where he could find her home, so he could start bringing back his memories from the neighborhood of Vicente López.

One day, he told her that he would call. It would be the first time in seventeen years they would hear each other's voices. So much time had gone by! Daniel was nervous. He had never called her during these two months of their e-mail reunion because the emotion was too intense after such a long time without seeing or talking to each other. Besides, he had left Argentina totally in love with her. His broken heart would not allow him to resist the feelings inside his soul.

Daniel had moved to the lakes district after his broken marriage. The chances of making a phone call from an old cell phone in those days—in such a remote place so far away from the capital city—were none. Moreover, a cell phone call to the other side of the world would have cost him a lot of money per minute and he couldn't afford it.

That Saturday, he went to visit his mother at her place in the center of Stockholm. After talking to her for a while, he went to a phone booth and called Clara.

"Hello," said Daniel

"Hello. Yes?" Clara answered.

"Clara?" said Daniel calmly

"Yes, who is it?" she asked.

"Hi Clara, it's Daniel. How are you?" he said. He waited for her to answer.

"Hi, Daniel! How are you doing? I cannot believe this," said Clara.

"Hi! Can you hear me properly?" he asked.

"Yes, I can hear you perfectly. How *are* you?" Clara asked this question with a steady voice, even though she was feeling fragile and vulnerable hearing Daniel's deep voice with his bit of a foreign accent. He pronounced words in a short and rigid way.

"I am fine, beautiful. I can't believe I am speaking to you," he said.

"Yes, it's true. It's so strange. I can't believe it either!" she said, her voice cracking for a second from the strong emotion she felt.

Then, silence ...

Daniel cleared his throat and continued to speak, despite his nervousness.

"Well, baby, looks like the day I go back to Argentina is getting closer. What do you think?" asked Daniel.

"I feel very, very flattered and I can't wait to see you," said Clara.

"You are going to be disappointed. I'm old," he said.

"I don't think so. Besides, I am in love with the person inside you, so even if you are old, or fat or bald—who cares?" replied Clara.

"You are really sweet, did you know that? Listen! I will call you tomorrow and let you know the exact date and we'll decide how to meet by e-mail. Okay?" Daniel said.

"Yes! It sounds good!"

"Ok, beautiful, we'll talk later," he said.

"Yes, later. Bye-bye," said Clara.

"I'll call you," he repeated.

"Okay, I will be waiting for your call," murmured Clara.

Clara hung up the phone and sat down. "No … no … no. I can't believe it! He called me! I heard his voice. He has such a sexy deep voice!

Suddenly, the phone rang again. It was him telling her that he had been so immersed in all of the excitement that he had forgotten to tell her something. She was so stunned and flattered that he made her feel like she was nineteen again. Daniel made sure she never forgot how beautiful he believed she was. That night Clara had vivid dreams.

More Letters

To: daniel@lovemail.com
From: clara@lovemail.com

Hi handsome,

Wow! All those kisses you sent over the phone …There are times when I just close my eyes and I think about you and I feel this incredible closeness. This must be like that feeling you told me about, when you can feel as if you can actually touch me. I have the feeling as if something goes all over my body but without touching me. It's like an energy that surrounds me. It's like your desire is so powerful that it expresses in me that way. It's very weird, because I explain it and it sounds really romantic. But it's not something I can just put into words. "I felt it that way, I could feel it around my body." And I think that it is not an easy thing to believe in.

When are you coming? I can't believe it! I live in Lisandro de la Torre street.

Don't you even think about dropping by as a surprise! After 17 years I have to go to the hair salon, the plastic surgeon, I have to buy myself a wig, change my apron and my broom, they are both old news!

I Love You.
Clara.

♥

It was so amazing that if Clara had to tell somebody about it, they would have thought she was crazy. Only a quantum physicist would have understood the feeling of being considered a crazy person. Right there, she didn't know much about being in two places at the same time. Of course, it all sounded so insane. Only physicists would call themselves crazy, looking at the fun side of the stuff that goes on in their minds as they discovered some new, weird knowledge.

For them it would be easy to understand the possibility of somebody feeling next to a person even if they were in two different and distant places.

We are energy; we belong to this universe. We are part of it. Each one of us is a little piece of universe. We communicate and connect at an unseen level. And that is what Clara and Daniel felt—and what kept them united for so long. They were deeply connected, in spite of the fact that one of them was in the northern hemisphere and the other one was in the southern hemisphere. It was this connection that drew them to each other in real life.

The Day is Coming.

To: clara@lovemail.com
From: daniel@lovemail.com
Subject: The day is coming.

Hi goddess!

I am so happy you liked my kisses. What about my nibbles? What do you think about getting together on September 19th or 20th? We have to decide what to do. Should I pick you up at your place or would you like to meet somewhere else? One of my brothers lives in Buenos Aires and is coming to the airport, so your coming too would be too much emotion for me. I believe I arrive on the 18th and I will stay up to October 10th. Think about it and let me know. I have to stop by at Bahía Blanca, but that would be a two-day stop. Nobody knows we are in contact; the only one who knows I am coming is you. I am going to see your dress and hold you tight. So, how should we do this? I am buying the ticket today. I'll let you know how everything went on as soon as I do it.

I LOVE YOU.
Daniel.

To daniel@lovemail.com
From: clara@lovemail.com
Re: The day is coming

Hi Love,

I am waiting for you, my love. Is it true you are coming? I almost can't believe it! Whenever we are at home I will cater to you and wake you up with whatever you like most. What is it? Coffee? Tea? Do you like toast with butter and jam? I have some plum jam I made myself. How many spoonfuls of sugar do you take in your coffee?

Yours,
Clara.
♥

The Trip

To: clara@lovemail.com
From: daniel@lovemail.com
Subject: The trip

Hi doll!

Hmm, I'll have toast, plum jam and Clara by my side for breakfast. Hmm, I can't believe it. It's crazy!

I arrive on Saturday 25th, what do you think about getting together on Sunday around, I don't know … you decide: 5 or 6 p.m., or later? I'll pick you up and we'll go out, and we'll see how things develop, how about it? Keep in mind that I don't remember places exactly and I don't have any idea about an awesome place to go. I am in your hands, in every sense of the phrase. Plan whatever you'd like to do; I am sure I will like it too. I am staying up until October 14th. After that I have to return because of a doctor's appointment my job demands.

Take care,
I love you.
Daniel
♥

To: daniel@lovemail.com
From: clara@lovemail.com
Re: The trip

Hi Daniel,

Look, I don't know how to put into words the excitement I feel for your coming here. I wrote to you, I don't know, two months ago? And that was enough to erase 17 years of absence between us, and it was also enough for you to have the strong desire to come here, and for me to want to have you here in my arms. Sometimes I feel I am living a dream. At work they ask me what is going on, why I look so radiant. And today I lost my keys, which never happens to me, since I am so organized. But of course it's because I had some news today. I was a little bit distracted. I have you with me all the time. You are in my thoughts. And I can feel you under my skin. I believe that when you come—I mean, I am sure—I am going to feel like hugging you the moment I see you. That's why I would like us to meet somewhere else but my place, 'cause if you come home to pick me up I won't be able to be spontaneous with the whole neighborhood watching, plus there is always the possibility of somebody stopping by at that precise moment. I don't know: the kids, my parents …anyway, I would like that special moment to be only ours, and not to be interrupted by anything. If we are on the street or in a bar and there are thousands of people around, who cares!? Of course you'll come to my house later on. We'll decide it once we are together. We should think of an easy place for you to find. Maybe "The Coffee Store," at the corner of Villate and Maipú Avenue, remember? It is right next to the Presidential House. Let me know what you think and what "the Dragon" says will be done. I am also in your hands. I mean it.

Well, baby, about the dress I told you about—it's very simple, it shows my body shape. It's just that when I bought it, I was thinking about you and I wanted to save it only for you. Ok, baby, I send you all my love.

Clara

♥

Daniel read this last letter from Clara. He read it once again and still couldn't help being shocked. Was destiny sending some kind of sign letting them know that they should be together? That this could be *the time* for them?

Clara was at home thinking of what they had talked about on the phone before his trip. *We should think of an easy place for you to find*, Clara had said. She recalled what he had said about not remembering every place after seventeen years. So, Clara decided that the corner of Villate and Maipú was a good place to meet since he had lived in Martínez fairly close to the presidential house when he was single. And the coffee shop they had been to together was on that corner.

Daniel thought, *This is going to give me the chills. She wants us to meet at Villate and Maipú. And it was from that corner that I saw her for the last time before I left for Europe. It was exactly the same day when her grandmother had died. I was standing on that corner looking at her, and she didn't know … because I never crossed the street to talk to her! And that was the last time I saw her before coming to Sweden.*

How could Clara choose that place without knowing this?

Why were these coincidences happening? They could be coincidences, or they could be premonitory messages, messages from the souls. Maybe they were messages from other dimensions—trying to warn them that some events had to be this way.

These kinds of messages are meant to reinforce the idea that all of us have to be confident and have faith. Perhaps these messages explain that we should never lose hope in finding our soul mate. He or she does exist! But only some of us are lucky enough to find that person in this lifetime. And we shouldn't let our soul mate go.

They both continued writing until the day of the arrival. Daniel called her and let her know he had arrived all right and that he had met his brother at the airport, after so many years. Experiencing that moment—filled with emotion and memories, plus being back in his hometown—made him a bit nervous and sensitive. And he still had to meet up with the love of his life. That night he talked to his brother for hours until he fell asleep; he finally surrendered, willing to rest after his long flight. The following day he was going to get together with Clara.

He called her on Sunday and they changed the corner they were supposed to meet at. They decided to meet at San Martín and Maipú in Vicente López. Clara was nervous. She called a cab to take her to the place, but she decided to get out of the car one block away from their meeting place. She paid for the ride, got out of the car, and crossed the street. Slowly, she started to walk toward the corner where he would be waiting. At first she couldn't see him. As she got closer, she saw him looking around, searching for her. Suddenly, they saw each other. Clara tried to pretend nothing was happening, but a wave of emotion swept through her body, from which butterflies emerged as though they had been trapped for seventeen years. And now they had been brought to life and were delicately starting to fly.

She had a few more steps ahead before being next to him. He looked as excited and deeply moved as she was.

He started getting closer, confidently. And as soon as they saw each other up close, they smiled and hugged in a way that made all the time and space that had kept them apart simply disappear.

What a hug! Finally, they had that slow but strong hug—the one they had been waiting and wishing for. He couldn't believe her body was so close to his—so warm, strong, and cozy.

She sensed his manhood just by touching his shoulders, and she let herself go in his arms, delighted by the intoxicating feeling that came with grazing his face and neck.

This was the first time they had been so close physically. Instinctively, they sought each other's lips, to have that kiss they had been yearning for, a kiss they should have shared when they were kids and that they couldn't give to each other until now when they were forty years old.

It was crazy! He couldn't believe he was kissing his Clara.

Meanwhile, the world was spinning, and everything going on around them seemed to be part of a movie in which the streets were filled with people who appeared and faded away before them, without them even noticing.

She felt the attraction, the desire and love that surrounded them as they had their first kiss. Their mouths were wet, and his steady and determined lips brought heat into hers. All of her days were handed over to him in that kiss. It was the kiss they both had secretly wished for since the day he had seen her for the first time.

Their faces separated slowly and they looked into each other's eyes. He pushed a strand of hair away from her face, gently, and they both smiled in a soothing way that only they understood.

"You've come, my love," whispered Clara

"I love you, beautiful. You look prettier than I imagined," he said.

"You look the same!" said Clara, smiling.

"I have a bit of a belly. I'm old," added Daniel.

They smiled.

"You look really handsome," commented Clara.

"What have you planned, baby? I don't remember anything. I have to get used to it after so much time without returning," said Daniel.

"I made reservations, as you suggested, for tonight in a French restaurant in San Isidro. And if you are okay with it, we can go have a coffee first at John Bull on Libertador Avenue so we can talk. How about it?" asked Clara.

"Whatever my goddess says," Daniel replied.

Together—in ecstasy and astonished, but acting as if they had seen each other the month before—they enjoyed each other's company just like they had when they were kids and he took English lessons with her. The bond they had shared in those long conversations was intact. Two hours went by. They kept on talking in that coffee shop, and he gave her a present—a set of Dior perfumes. She gave him the scarf she'd been knitting since the moment he had told her he was coming.

When the time came for dinner they went to the restaurant and kept on talking. They felt so comfortable together. They talked about the letter, the wedding, his trip, his arrival in Sweden, children. They didn't talk much about their exes. They opened up to each other with sincerity, just like they had before.

At one point, he told her he had something to say to her but he was not sure if she was going to believe it. And that was how he let her know what had happened on that corner of Villate and Maipú, where she had suggested meeting for his arrival.

She could not believe it. Clara asked him why he didn't even say hi or come over to her. She remembered being at the door of the funeral parlor when her grandmother—la *Nonna*—had died. The funeral parlor was right in front of the presidential house in Olivos, very near that corner of Villate and Maipú. He told her that he was really hurt, and that he couldn't stand seeing her with somebody else. And that since he loved her so much, he thought the best thing was to let her be happy. So that had been the last time he saw her.

"And you chose that place for us to meet after seventeen years apart," Daniel said one more time.

"It's true," said Clara. "I chose that place without knowing this, just like you chose that song without knowing the premonition hidden in the lyrics," Clara said.

"Do you want to know another one?" Daniel asked.

"Yes, of course," she said, without letting him out of her sight as he spoke.

"Around three or four days after you wrote to me via mail to Sweden for the first time, I was with my mom in her flat in Stockholm watching a movie. The movie was about a couple getting together after lots of years of being apart. Suddenly, my mom said to me:

'You see, son? You don't have to lose hope.'

And I thought: *What is up with her now?*

"Listen to this please, Clara," said Daniel. He repeated his mother's words in astonishment: *Tell me, Daniel. Whatever happened to that girl—your English teacher? What was her name?*

"And I was so shocked!" added Daniel. "You had just written to me some days before, after seventeen years! It's like sorcery," he exclaimed.

"No! I can't believe it!" said Clara, her eyes wide open. "It's something that ...I don't know ..." Clara hesitated for a second. "But, how did your mom remember me? She didn't even meet me once! She and I must have spoken on the phone when you came to class one or maybe two times? I remember she was worried because you had just lost your father. She must have sensed, as a mother, that you loved me," Clara said.

"But the weird thing is that you guys never talked about you and me, and it is also strange that she remembered me the moment you were watching a movie of that genre! It is like an omen," said Clara.

He stared at her while she was talking.

Suddenly he said, "Yes, love. You are so beautiful! Shall we go?"

"Yes, sure," agreed Clara.

It was half past twelve at night. They both arrived at Clara's house.

An expectant silence filled the room that was already filled with love and desire. Together they walked around the ground floor of the house, where she showed him the place.

Once in the kitchen, she put the kettle on to make some coffee, but neither of them really wanted to drink it. He took her by the hand. He got closer to her and started to slowly push her, guiding her and making her step back a bit until she felt her back touch the kitchen counter. As he grabbed her waist he kissed her, allowing his love to erupt like the steaming magma of a volcano. She hugged him and kissed him passionately in return. The energy of his kiss went through her entire body making her shiver with desire. Daniel's mind was half gone as he enjoyed kissing Clara's eager mouth, caressing her warm body, discovering her shape and finding her curves leading to her femininity.

He was delighted as he caressed her with his mouth and hands in a way he never could before. They were isolated from the real world, united by the magic of the moment, and couldn't believe what was happening to them. They came back to reality only after a few minutes, when the boiling water generated steam out of the kettle's spout, making a musical sound.

They smiled, looked at each other, and Clara said, "Somebody has to turn the kettle off!"

Clara poured the coffee in mugs and brought them to the living room. They tried it, but both cups were still full when they decided to go upstairs. Coffee was a formality; they both knew they were finally going to be together after seventeen years.

They felt that even though they had spent the last five hours dining and chatting, time hadn't passed. It seemed as if they'd only been apart for two months; it was very strange.

Once in the bedroom, he took off the dress covering her body. He watched her body in the mirror, touching her with strong hands. They loved and surrendered to one another.

They gave each other everything they had been saving, carefully cherished in their souls. They showed their love to each other all along their bodies in a slow and hot ritual that lasted all night. She gave in to his masculinity, and he allowed her to release a dose of love—looking deep into her feelings and her skin—until six in the morning when they were too tired to keep going. They finally fell asleep, their mouths marked on each corner of the other one's body, wrapped in their love.

From that day on, Daniel would take turns seeing Clara, his brothers, family and friends. One night he told Clara how the meeting had gone with his good friend Omar. Without Omar having any idea, Daniel went to his house one day and rang the bell. Omar opened the peephole of the door that looked into the street. It was one of those big antique wooden doors.

"Yes?" said Omar.

"Hello, good afternoon," answered Daniel.

"Good afternoon," said Omar. "How can I help you?" he asked.

Daniel was really enjoying himself seeing his buddy after such a long time and not being recognized, so he kept on going with the conversation.

"Is this Omar Darcy's house?" asked Daniel.

"Yes, it's me," said Omar.

"Yes it's me," repeated Daniel. "Have you already forgotten me?"

Omar opened the door, looked at him and shouted, "No, it can't be! Son of a bitch! How can you do this to me, brother?"

Omar went outside. They hugged in a heartfelt way. Omar looked at Daniel and hugged him again. He couldn't believe Daniel was right in front of him. So many years had gone by since he had last seen his friend!

"Are you planning to kill me? I am going to suffer from a heart attack! How can you show up this way? You are *crazy* man, come on, come inside," said Omar laughing.

They were both smiling. Omar said in a loud voice: "Marcela! Come! Look who's here!"

Another night Clara heard the story of the time Daniel showed up in a pub his cousin used to work in and started talking to him. Daniel was sitting at the bar counter until the hugging and surprises began. The reunions were unforgettable. Incredibly happy times would remain in his memory ever after.

Unfortunately, the day when Daniel would have to leave came sooner than expected. From that moment, their lives were going to change. Each day they spent together was a delight until the time came to say goodbye. He had to go back to Sweden. He promised to return.

Clara and Daniel were together in bed.

"You know what?" said Clara.

"What, baby?" he replied.

"We don't have to cry. We have to be strong and make the most of these last hours we have together before you leave. They will give us strength for the next time you come," Clara whispered in his ear.

A deep silence floated in the air.

They were holding each other and looking into each other's eyes. He caressed her hair while he looked at her. He listened to her speaking in silence. She looked at him deep in his eyes, trying to record in her mind that look, full of feelings.

"Sure, we are going to be strong. I know I can count on you. I have lots of stuff to solve, but I will be back, I know it," said Daniel firmly.

"I love you so much, my love," said Clara, her voice filled with emotion.

He stared into her soul and said, in a really low voice, soft, almost inaudibly, "I've loved you for twenty-six years, and I never forgot you during all this time, not even one day. I will come back to you."

Chapter 5

Barriers

When we think of a barrier, we generally envision something physical, a material thing that stops us from trespassing or from crossing a boundary.

This is the case for most people's first attempt to define the word.

Physical barriers are necessary to maintain order in society as well as to protect people from dangerous things. However, there is one kind of barrier that cannot be seen. Emotional barriers are usually self-made, and they impede us from going forward due to a hidden fear. Although this fear is unconscious, we can change our point of view to be more aware of the possibilities that lie ahead of us.

Daniel had made such a great effort to adapt to a culture that was so different from his that he was afraid of losing all the emotionally valuable things he had achieved after so many years.

As an immigrant, Daniel had found it difficult to get a good job in Sweden. He loved motorbikes and had learned a lot about them in Argentina when he was a young boy. Due to his knowledge, he had been able—after trying many other jobs—to get a post as a seller in a shop for a well-known motorbike brand. Although he was a very responsible worker, being a foreigner did not make things easier for him to obtain a higher salary. He was in charge of his children. And at this point, after being separated for the second time, his ex-wife was not helping him in any way. Needless to say, she was trying to force him to go back with her. Of course, this attitude was not apparent. She was secretly doing whatever she could to spoil his decisions.

When Daniel met her for the first time, she didn't really catch his attention.

Some days passed, and Daniel's brother told him he was inviting a colleague of his wife to dinner. George's wife, Svetlana, was Swedish. She worked as a secretary in a well-known car factory. She spent some time every day talking to the girl who helped deliver food at the restaurant where she often had lunch. Her name was Paola Isabel. She was not tall, had dark hair, and had a slight Latin accent when she spoke Swedish. But she spoke it quite well, taking into account that she came from Peru and did not know a word of Swedish when she arrived in the country.

Paola Isabel seemed to be a nice young girl. She was twenty-two years old and had arrived in Sweden some years before trying to escape from her past. Her cute little boy, who was almost six when she met Daniel, was her motivation to live and struggle in a country she did not know well. Paola seemed to be sweet and charming, but she was hiding a secret that had turned her resentful against life. Her appearance was that of a pretty young ordinary girl, but her cold light blue eyes revealed a weird, sharp expression.

A month had passed since Daniel's arrival to Sweden. He was running out of time, as he would have to leave the country in another two months. That night, dinner was ready at Daniel's brother's apartment in the poor area of Stockholm, a piece of land set aside for people coming from abroad. Only the Swedish could access other important areas of this wonderful city. And, although George had married a Swedish girl, he had a job as a painter and did not have a good salary. Svetlana's family had never belonged to the high Swedish society. So they managed their lives according to what George could make for a living.

Svetlana opened the door as soon as the bell rang. Paola stepped inside. The women exchanged some words at the entrance. Soon the four of them were having a good time around the table, engaged in a conversation in fluent Spanish, as three spoke Spanish perfectly well and Svetlana had learned some Spanish in school.

When Daniel met Paola Isabel for the first time that night, he found her charming and talkative, although he did not like her much. But his brother convinced him that dating her would be a good way to find an opportunity to stay in Sweden.

They started going out together. Paola needed a husband and a father for her son. She told Daniel that her son's father had left them when they were in Perú and that they had never seen him again.

Daniel was sad, on the other side of the world, and felt he had no chance to have the love of his life with him as she had already gotten married. Soon Daniel would have to leave Sweden.

On a dark, cold Swedish night, Daniel and Paola came to an agreement to help each other. Paola had already obtained Swedish nationality, and by offering to marry Daniel, neither of them would have to leave Sweden. As the years passed, she gained weight and started feeling even more frustrated. This encouraged her evil and acid personality to show up. And every day Daniel discovered the real woman behind his wife. She was always demanding things from him and complaining about money. Instead of valuing her husband, she criticized him and minimized his great efforts to develop and sustain their family. They had two boys together.

Even Paola's son—whom Daniel adopted and gave his surname to—was aware of his mother being so rude to Daniel. But Daniel's own children witnessed a father who was constantly minimized and not respected. Paola became more aggressive, but in a subtle way she showed another personality when she wanted to obtain something. She praised him whenever she wanted to get something for her benefit.

Paola was a sharp observer who could catch at a glance any weakness in other people's personalities. She used it to manipulate her husband, victimizing herself. She even went so far as to invent an illness to make him feel guilty in case he eventually decided to leave her. She believed herself to be so powerful that many people would say she was conceited, even when she did not have any special gift to justify this perception of herself. In a way, her selfishness did not allow her to realize she was destroying him.

She had told him lies to obtain what she wanted. Daniel was suffering from this kind of attitude, but wasn't aware of her lies. He felt hidden threats behind her kind words. He was afraid of losing his children if he left her. But in time, he would realize this would turn out to be his best decision.

Sometimes it isn't others who limit us. It is a question of choosing the right path. This is something we need to learn while we live. Limits and barriers are usually put on us by *ourselves* because we are afraid of doing something. Making the right decision is entirely our own choice. We need to realize that in this life *we* decide what we choose.

Chapter 6

The Dragon, the Tigress, the Angel

Daniel had left. Clara was filled with pleasure but sad about being separated again. This was not going to be easy. What were they going to do to be together, and how? How could they move to be near each other? Their children were involved. How were they going to do it? It was quite a desperate feeling, but the strength of their love pushed them to continue against all odds—as though they had to swim across the Atlantic Ocean.

They were only focused on thinking of each other, something they did spontaneously. Each day, most of the time—without thinking of it deliberately—he was thinking of her and she was thinking of him. They started seeing certain signs manifesting in different ways at precise moments, confirming the presence of the other one. These signs appeared in the form of messages on the radio or on television, on an advertisement in the street, in a magazine, in a book, or in a conversation with somebody else.

One day out of the blue he called her and told her, "Do you know what happened to me today? I was in a bookshop looking for a book and I took one by chance. I opened it in the middle so as to have a look at it inside and on the page I opened it there was your name. I read *Clara* ... I couldn't believe it!" said Daniel.

Phone calls and letters started again.

To: clara@lovemail.com
From: daniel@lovemail.com
Subject: Dreaming of you

Hi beauty:

Did I tell you that yesterday I dreamt of you? I felt so well after talking to you, I had a dream full of love and kisses. I dreamt of all the kisses I gave you and you gave me. It was such a real dream that when I woke up I was sure I had loved you and kissed you, I had made everything to you until you whispered that phrase I love that is only ours. What a dream! I woke up in delight but I realized it was just a dream and ... well ... I didn't like it because I couldn't hug you and go to sleep again.

I have never been so close to someone in spite of the distance, do you understand? I love everything about you, your eyes, your heart, your hair, your smile, your deep look, your skin, your eyebrows, your legs, your back, your bra, your size of shoes ... everything. I love you the way you are. With me you have to be as you are. I want you to be Clara, I want you mostly to feel well with me. I feel and I want to make you good, in a way that you feel comfortable, free. In a way in which you can grow as a person and I by your side, to support you and see that you are happy. I want you, and I will make whatever is needed in spite of this provisional distance, to be sure that the love I feel for you is the most real.

I want to learn to love you, to know you, because our souls need our love the most. Both of us, only you and I, can feed our love day by day, not ever letting it fade away, because, without knowing, we have both done it during all these years and, in spite of not being together as a couple, we have been more united than anyone. That is something neither of us will be able to forget. I am faithful about us and despite all the difficulties we are going to encounter I WILL ALWAYS BE BY YOUR SIDE.

My soul united to my heart, which are full of you, will make this last forever …

And I want you to be absolutely sure that, what I wrote in the letter: "Today or Tomorrow" will make Tomorrow become Forever with you my Clara. I Love you, love … LOVE.

Your LOVE, crazy about you, my goddess.
Daniel.

♥

Clara answered:

To: daniel@lovemail.com
From: clara@lovemail.com
Subject: Re: The trip

Love, we will never look for because we are united forever, that's to say we have ALWAYS been, so nothing and nobody will be able to separate us because, in a way, we are more than united. I want you to know that I feel something which is very nice and that turns into a pleasant sensation. It is that I feel you by my side all the time. When I tell you that I take you with me everywhere I mean that without realizing it, I am always thinking of you.

Today, for example, I taught early in the morning at home and afterward I devoted some time to reading on a sofa in the calmness of the living room. Something that I cannot frequently do, and while I was reading, "Soul Mates," I could feel as if you were sitting beside me (I swear to God—I don't know how to explain it, but that is what I feel).

It is just like as when you wrote to me, telling me that you have never felt so close to somebody in spite of the distance. It must be the willingness I feel of being with you—or the years we have been separated—that make me think of giving you all that I could not give you so far. I feel I want you to be happy, I want to take care of you. And it is because of that, as you say, that we have to be strong and we are surely going to make it happen. We have to do things well, especially for our children, because we are not alone. Count on me, I want you to know that I am waiting for you and that you are the one and only owner.

Let's see my love, do you remember when we went to the apartment? Anything is ok with us, even a small bed. And, it sounded funny when you said just talking about yourself: "Have a look at him buddy, who would have ever imagined this?" Do you know what? You have to tell your friend there in Sweden, the doctor—Ramiro— the one you told about us and our reencounter, that I have been to the ophthalmologist and he found that I have a weird problem, not very often found ... and it is that besides seeing what anybody else sees I can see the inner part of people and when I saw you I instantly fell in love with you. Not only because you are handsome, but because of the transparency of your soul. I have never seen that before, and will never ever see it in anybody else. I send you one of those kisses ... I

LOVE YOU.
Clara

To: clara@lovemail.com
From: daniel@lovemail.com
Subject: Sincere love
Hellooo!

Such beautiful words! You are going to make me cry with emotion ...You are divine, you are a real GODDESS, goddess of LOVE. You are the only person that has made me feel so well since we met when I was sixteen and you still continue doing it now that I am forty one, it's crazy! I LOVE YOU, I am mad about you, you mean everything to me. I must tell you that what you told me about feeling me beside you has happened to me several times … it's so crazy! One night I woke up as I was dreaming about you and I felt you hugging me, it was super real … so much so that it gave me chills … I don't know, difficult to explain … I LOVE YOU like crazy, but true balanced and sincere love, without the games, you know? Yeah?

I adore you. I love you … if you didn't pick up on it.

I was thinking about something someone told me a while ago. You can have every material possession you have taken away, even your body. But no one would ever be able to take away from you the person you have in your heart and whom you think about.

NO ONE will be able to take the place you have in my heart.

Yours always,
Daniel.
♥

They say that the power of the mind is immeasurable, that what you think can be turned into reality, if you really believe in it; Daniel was doing that. He had thought of Clara every single day when he was in Sweden; he had thought of her constantly, and it had helped him achieve his dream. She reciprocated his feelings, and Daniel confirmed that he had also felt her presence. Could it be that their souls were united? United in such a way that neither space nor distance could separate them?

But they had to do something to be able to be together from that moment on. Did they have to do something, or just send a sign to the universe asking that their dream come true? They had to have faith in the fact that what had happened in their lives was for some incomprehensible reason—just as there was a reason they had reunited after such a long time, and just as there was a destiny, a time and space for the two of them.

They only had to believe, not to doubt. In a way, the universe had already demonstrated to them that nothing was impossible, that miracles do exist.

Clara perceived Daniel's love in each word, and she answered with her heart. Together—with their words—they celebrated their reunion.

To: clara@lovemail.com
From: daniel@lovemail.com
Subject: Our souls are together

Hello, I send you kisses ... send me a "Hello." I miss you a lot ... I want to see you ... hug you ... I want to be with you. Look at you, listen to you, what is it that is going on with me? Would I be in love? Would that be the reason why I see you everywhere and everything I see reminds me of you? Do you feel my soul next to yours?

Love you,
Daniel

Clara could also feel his soul next to hers. She could feel him in the same way Daniel had explained—that when he was dreaming of her one night, he woke up feeling her hand caressing his back. This was weird and moving, because if Daniel or Clara or any person who had experienced something similar dared to tell it to anyone else, their comment would have been rejected. People would have stared at them with pity, thinking: *It's obvious. He is so much in love with her that he believes she is caressing him.*

Daniel did not believe anything, and neither did Clara. They started to believe that *it could be possible* now that they had gone through the experience.

It was after this experience that Clara started considering the possibility of a special communication between two people who had such a powerful bond. It was a kind of communication that attached them to each other in both time and space.

They were connected in a space beyond the physical place we know. A bonding space that keeps twin souls united, even though they exist in separate and different physical levels.

In that way, they kept on feeding their souls with their eternal love, kept in a box or at the bottom of the heart.

One day, Clara found a book by an English author named Diana Cooper, *Vislumbrando a los Ángeles.*

Here is the author's explanation:

"Angels are superior spiritual beings. Most of human beings are spirits of lower evolution that are in a physical body to live this experience on the Earth and that everything and everybody are made out of vibrations. The denser the vibration, the denser the object, that's why we can see and touch the chairs, tables and humans. Angels are in a much more elevated level than us. Among them there are some dedicated to sanity, some others to peace and others to give love.

The fact that we are before the presence of angels opens the doors to our consciousness to bigger and higher possibilities. And they are among us now much more than in any other period in history. Because planet Earth has reached a turning point. We have plundered our planet and we have surrounded it with an almost impenetrable force. Our creator has stated that this cannot continue. They are not going to allow us to destroy this beautiful planet because it would lead to unbalance the Universe.

Most frequently, angels are invisible for us, because they vibrate in a level which is beyond our visual field. Sometimes we can elevate our awareness high enough so as to see them … Generally what we feel is their presence and an impulse of energy that comes from somewhere to help us …

When angels visit humans, they feel a moving sensation of love and peace. Angels come to tranquilize us and give us the impulse to go on."

Reading this excerpt made it clear to Clara what had happened to her when she felt that impulse to write to Daniel.

So, when people say "An angel came from heaven"—they mean it! It had happened to her, and it had happened to many other people as well. We have to be more alert to the signs.

We must call the angels for them to be able to assist us.

Many people make fun of this because they feel ashamed or are afraid to admit it's possible. These people are immersed in traditional logical thinking. But we need the stimulation and great wisdom of what connects us with our right hemisphere of the brain. We need it in order to be open to a more spiritual world, something the current generation desperately needs.

From then on, Clara knew this possibility existed and that if we called them, angels would come help us.

Daniel knew Clara had felt a very strong impulse. A special energy had guided her to look for him, to tell him what she could never tell him before.

They continued writing and deepening their love, even though they were separated by oceans—as it was written in the song. They were more united than ever before, in spite of the distance and time.

And Daniel wrote:

To: clara@lovemail.com
From: daniel@lovemail.com
Subject: Only you know me

Maybe there's a silent time … a time with only a few letters, it won't be because I do not want to write to you or I do not want to listen to you … maybe it is because I cannot make things in a more organized or planned way … but it is so crazy! It opposes the state in which we are. A state of Love.

This state or this energy that you do not plan, you only feel it and it is so strong that it does not allow us to think consequently, you feel and react.

At this moment and since I've met you, I could always be myself and show me as I really am, only you know me, only with you I could be transparent, I could give you all my love without keeping anything in case I was hurt. With you everything is so different, it's a dream come true. If I had to look for a synonym to the word love that would be Clara. It's you who, after such a long time of being covered by ice, could melt it from the moment you sent your first mail and since I saw you at San Martín and Maipú …

That kiss, our first kiss … I will never ever forget as well as our first six hours or so. It was wonderful to feel I was inside you and to feel I was loving in a way I couldn't ever love before! They are moments that will remain forever carved in my heart and soul.

And what makes me feel better is to know that that astonishing woman called Clara, is not only the love of my life but also my twin soul.

And in the future I only hope and dream she would be my woman for the rest of my life …

I love you,
Daniel
♥

To: daniel@lovemail.com
From: clara@lovemail.com
Subject: TODAY and ALWAYS

TODAY. Today I want you to be more balanced and calm than ever … really the way you are … the way I see you. Today I want to tell you that I'll always be with you, to caress you, to accompany you, to be by your side, the way I like. That same way we know when we are together. That's to say, ALWAYS, because we are always together.

Today I will softly run my fingers on your skin, over your whole body in a warm love caress … to strengthen you and please you.

I LOVE you,
Clara
♥

To: clara@lovemail.com
From: daniel@lovemail.com
Subject: RP TODAY and ALWAYS

Today and ALWAYS … I have so many things to give you, I have my soul and my heart that are already yours. I belong to you. You are everything to me. Yesterday I dreamt again of you … a dream full of love, I could feel your skin, your body becoming one with mine.

I love you,
Daniel
♥

Daniel pressed the *send* icon and immediately after doing it he wrote another e-mail:

To: clara@lovemail.com
From: daniel@lovemail.com
Subject: RP TODAY and ALWAYS

Hello, how much I LOVE you! I cannot stop dreaming about our next meeting. I love you the way I have never loved someone, and that is because I only loved you all of my life.

Daniel.
♥

Clara and Daniel realized that the strength of their physical communication was due to their spiritual union. This strength was born in their souls and taken to their bodies, provoking this special ecstasy they shared.

To: clara@lovemail.com
From: daniel@lovemail.com
Subject: A nightmare

Do you know that each time I open the e-mail and see 0 messages I feel sad. But when I see "you've got a message" it is enough for me if you only write a few words. And you ... Do you feel the same? Yesterday I had a nightmare that I sent you an e-mail and your address did not exist. I couldn't contact you on the phone ... It was horrible!

Daniel
♥

To: daniel@lovemail.com
From: clara@lovemail.com
Subject: A love like this one ...

Daniel,

Do not suffer my love ... Do not think about negative possibilities, because a love like this one, that lasted in time and in spite of anything. A love that lasted in spite of our ex couples, in spite of having suffered the fact of being separated ... A love like this one does not die. It does not end, it does not fall.

Think of what you told me about thinking of me each day of your life, when you had that break at lunch time. The one Swedish call "fika" as you taught me. Each single day you were thinking of me ... You thought about what I would be doing ... if I was happy ...

And I thought about you each night … what it had been of your life … If you continued driving motorbikes … This is incredible!

Can't you see that we are, we have been, and we will always be connected through our thoughts?

A deep emotion is running through my veins right now. Do not suffer please. Think about how much we love each other. Think it is possible that a woman loves you so much … that she does not want to be with anybody else. I Love You.

Clara

♥

It was incredible to think that they had loved each other for so long without having any kind of contact. They hadn't touched each other, seen each other, talked to each other, shared daily activities, made love, laughed together, or cried together.

Daniel had planned to come back in four months, but the trip had to be put off, making the reunion seem so far away. It would be eight months until they would be able to see each other again.

To: daniel@lovemail.com
From: clara@lovemail.com
Subject: I miss you so much

This is going to drive me crazy … I cannot stand it any longer, I miss you so much! It is too difficult to be separated. But what is weird, at the same time, is that both of us are ok. I mean, after not seeing each other for more than seven months, waiting for this moment seems to be an eternal torture. And, at the same time, we become aware that our relationship, the bond that ties us, is so strong that it makes neither of us surrender. Both of us can bear the physical separation because the bond of our souls is stronger. I feel that what makes us feel so well is the way we communicate.

This is something not easily found in somebody else's body. It can only be given to you by the person you feel that bond with. And this emotion filled with love is transmitted to our bodies when we make love.

Clara

♥

Suddenly the telephone rang and Clara picked up the receiver. It was Daniel who had just finished reading her e-mail.

"Yes my goddess, it is exactly like this," said Daniel from the northern hemisphere. "I feel exactly the same. You cannot imagine how much I miss you … this is also driving me crazy. I want to be there right now … where are you?" he asked anxiously.

"I am in my bed," said Clara.

"Mmm … delicious. Can I get in there with you?" he asked.

"Of course, honey … for sure I let you stay with me. How much I miss you!" murmured Clara.

All of a sudden silence could be perceived floating in the air; it was delicate but stunning at the same time. Daniel needed those seconds to be able to continue talking.

She was on the other side in silence as well. Those seconds seemed eternal. However, the delay of hearing each other was calm and free of sadness.

They knew they were counting on that moment of silence because they could not find words to express what they felt for each other.

Suddenly, without letting her start talking, he said:

"Hello, beautiful."

"Hello, sweet," answered Clara.

"Do you have an idea of what I am going to do to you now?" he asked.

"Uhh … no, I don't know," replied Clara.

"I am going to fill your body with kisses 'til you beg me please to stop. I am going to caress your skin with my hands running along each bend of your shapes … mmm … your skin. How is it that you have such soft skin? It has such a special texture. I was always attracted by your skin, imagine now that I could enjoy it!" he added.

"Love, I also fall for your skin … I let my fingers run over your shoulders softly reaching your face. I caress your beard and start moving my fingers softly and slowly apart from your face … So, as you wish my caress, you follow the movement of my hand that keeps moving apart and guides you close to me until your mouth reaches mine …" said Clara in soft sexy voice.

"Mmm … I like it … yes like this just as if there was a magnet in between our mouths," Daniel imagined what she was describing.

"Do you like it?" asked Clara.

"Yes! Keep on telling me," he pleaded.

"So then, our mouths unite in a passionate kiss, like the one we shared at San Martín and Maipú," Clara was recalling that moment.

"Yes! My tongue caresses your mouth, that mouth of yours that can drive me so crazy," said Daniel.

"That mouth only belongs to you. It only wants to be with you. I am so much in love with you. I want you to tell me about that book you read which had love stories," Clara said.

"Aha … you liked the idea!" added Daniel conspicuously.

"Yes, you left me wondering about it … the other day when you phoned," Clara said in a mock recriminating tone.

"Okay I'm gonna tell you, but I don't know if it was exactly like this …" he said.

So Daniel started telling her what he had read:

"The dragon and the tigress went together to a party. He was wearing a black suit and an impeccably white shirt. The tie matched the color of his eyes. She was wearing a black dress totally covering her chest up to the neck. It had no sleeves. It tightened her body … there was no neckline. The dress only allowed the legs to be seen from her knees downwards, letting her perfect feet stand out. She was wearing a pair of silver high heeled shoes. The cloth adhered to the bends of her body, covering it almost completely but making it look suggestive. There was no need to show anything to anyone … The reason was that she was setting all apart for her dragon."

"Do you like it?" asked Daniel.

"Yes sure, do not stop. Continue telling me," said Clara.

"Once at the party they mixed among people … they talked, greeted friends and acquaintances. From time to time they separated and they looked around for each other. She approached him, slowly walking round in circles. She blinked an eye to him. He answered with a smile while he kept on talking. But, from time to time he looked at her with his green eyes almost mesmerizing her with *love*.

She suggestively lured her prey in slow motion. He started burning on fire and left the circle of people he had been talking to with a polite excuse. He looked for something to drink and gave it to her, holding her by her waist and pulling her body close to him. He firmly tightened his grip on her, dominant. He offered her the drink and kissed her on her cheek, his lips leaving a mark on her skin as his beard barely brushed against it. She approached his ear with her lips and whispered in a sexy voice, "When you look for me and cannot find me, it will be because I will be waiting for you in the gardens … do you agree?"

He answered, "Will I have to take care?" She said, "Yes, beware because you don't know what can happen to you outside there.

They smiled in shared complicity and looked deep into each other's eyes in an endless instant that deepened inside like a black hole in outer space. They went to sit at the table and had dinner. After that, they talked to the rest of the guests at their table and danced together slowly and embraced."

"Aha," said Clara, listening attentively.

Daniel went on talking:

"He stopped his hand at the bottom of her back ... she released her left arm by her side as she perceived his hand holding her waist. Then she sensually and delicately moved her fingers at the back of his neck, playing with his hair. Their faces were close. Their heads leaned against each other. Some minutes of ecstasy passed by when, suddenly she stepped back and sensually started moving her body in front of him, softly changing her movements before him, turning her back on him as he watched. He enjoyed the love his tigress was giving him with each provocative movement. Others watching seemed envious because they could not hide the love they felt for one another. Consequently, their dance became an erotic attraction for the ones watching them.

They went back to the table, and she left the room without him noticing it. It was then, after some minutes, when he looked for her but could not find her around. Therefore, he went directly to the garden.

A huge park with low hills surrounded the mansion. It was filled with small bushes and pine trees, forming like a little forest.

He saw her standing on the steps of wide, long, marble stairs that led to the park. He quickly went down to reach her. He held her tight, close to his body as he looked for her mouth and kissed her. Both melted, their mouths in a deep kiss looking for their souls, swimming in a sweet, erotic contact.

Afterward, they walked together till they reached a far corner surrounded with trees and bushes, though once inside they could not be seen. Mmm ... what have they planned? There they started a ritual full of kisses and caresses that—"

Daniel stopped himself. "Do you like it my goddess?" he said in a soft deep voice.

"Of course. my love. Please keep on telling me," said Clara.

Daniel went on with his story, and they stayed for more than an hour on the phone till they said goodnight to each other as if they were side by side on the same bed.

"Are you going to tell me more next time?" asked Clara.

"Do not doubt it, beautiful," replied Daniel.

"Till tomorrow, handsome," she said.

"Till tomorrow, honey. Have a good night."

The piano keys transmitted powerful vibrations full of messages. The air acquired strength while the rhythm increased. "Angelfire" by the American keyboardist Josiah Barlow—Clara's favorite song—sounded powerfully and delicately at the same time, framing her thoughts.

What seemed incredible was that in spite of being so far away from each other, they felt so much closer. It was due to the communication they shared in every aspect; that is what kept them united. It was because they had thought for so much time about each other; this had kept them united even when they did not have any contact at all—even when they didn't talk on the phone or write to each other. It was something that would always keep them united, despite any circumstance. It was true now more than ever, now that they had experienced the vibrant emotion of sharing all that communication in body and soul.

Chapter 7

San Nicolás

Yes! The moment to meet again had come! Finally, after eight months, they could be together once more.

So, they arranged a meeting.

"Hi, baby. How is the most beautiful woman in Argentina doing? I'm sorry, in the *world*," said Daniel on the phone.

"Come on, don't lie! You must say the same thing to every girl out there," said Clara.

"Yes, I have two blondes right here that seem to believe me. Ha ha," laughed Daniel.

"Don't say that! Sometimes we say things just kidding and they end up being super real," exclaimed Clara.

"Oh, really? And how's that?" Daniel asked.

"Let me tell you. My father had a coworker in his office that every Saturday after lunch he left his house with some excuse and said to his wife: 'Bye, I'm going to my mistress's house.' And he laughed. And his wife always said goodbye to him with a smile on her face and said, 'Okay, have fun! Ha ha ha!' And they always made that *joke*. Do you follow me?" asked Clara.

"Yes, I'm listening, beautiful," answered Daniel.

"Okay, so the story repeated itself Saturday after Saturday, for years. Until one day the wife got a phone call. Guess who it was. It was the mistress, to let her know that her husband had died," exclaimed Clara.

"No!" Daniel said, almost shouting in surprise.

"Yes! The guy had a heart attack at her house. Can you believe it?" said Clara.

"It went kinda bad for the guy. I'm going to have to be careful. Ha ha! No, leaving all kidding aside. Poor woman, what a horrible way to find out so many lies," added Daniel.

"Yeah, now I know you are with two Swedish blondes, one at each side of you, right? Ha ha," said Clara.

"Yeah, and I have two Norwegians waiting by the door," said Daniel.

"Okay baby, I don't want to steal time from those girls. Will you let me know when you arrive?" said Clara jokingly.

"Yes, darling, that was why I called you. Next Thursday I'll be right there. I already talked to Gerardo, who is going to pick me up at the airport. Then I'll have a little nap to regain strength for my goddess, because the jetlag kills me, and I will see you Thursday afternoon in San Martin and Maipú?" said Daniel.

"Love it, it is super romantic. Of course I want to meet you again in that corner. It's like re-experiencing the day we met, where we had our first kiss," murmured Clara.

"Hmm," Daniel´s voice sounded sexy. "Oh, beautiful, I can't wait to see you. Your mouth ..."

"It's waiting for you, my love," Clara said.

Seeing each other again was like re-living their last reunion on that same corner. How many times had they passed that corner as kids without imagining the importance it would have one day in their lives? How many people walk through places that will one day become spaces of convergence in their lives? Meeting again charged them with desire, hope, certainty, sensuality, perseverance, strength, and the power of love.

And the story repeated itself, just like eight months before—only this time they skipped coffee and dinner. Talk? They had already talked enough. Now they were hungry for each other. They needed to feed from one another to make up for all the time their souls fed from the agony of waiting for their loved one.

This time they had more time to spend together. Daniel didn't have to visit as many people as he did the first time back to Argentina. In fact, he did anyway, but not with the same haste, anxiety, lost time, and emotions as before. Emotions did take over him when he visited his father's grave after eighteen years. At the same time, it made that strong and determined man a little bit tougher. His love for Clara had made him go back to his roots, to his past, his friends, brothers, and his land, Argentina. But mostly, it made him develop stronger feelings for Clara. It made him want to share more and more time with the woman of his life who gave him everything—all those things she couldn't give him before, and she asked for nothing in return.

She was really worried about his health; she knew he wouldn't complain about it. He was very strong and suffered in silence. In Sweden, he had been given a bunch of medications as a solution to his disease. Probably the same thing would have happened here. But what would happen if his soul were healed with all the love that he couldn't get before? What would happen if he allowed his body to be filled with true love, if he took love pills and warm massages charged with desire? What could he lose? Who could be hurt by this?

They spent the most beautiful days and nights in Buenos Aires, and they even went to the beach for a few days.

The trees that surrounded the cabins in Mar de las Pampas next to the Atlantic coast were leafy and picturesque, similar to the ones that Daniel had next to his house in Sweden. The only difference was that back there in Sweden, water looked like mirrors.

On hot days the sun stared at the sand as if it wanted to devour it. The hours they spent together were hot too. They stayed in their cabin sharing their love while the waves of the Argentine sea went wild, splashing vibrant, energetic, and sensual foam that was full of life. The water seemed to want to reflect some of this love story that was taking place in front of it.

They enjoyed sharing a few days under the same roof.

They would say each other's names aloud just to make sure they weren't dreaming. They would call each other from another room to check to see if it really was the other person.

The walks they took and the deep, honest conversations they had brought them closer and closer.

They went back to Buenos Aires and visited Daniel's dear friend, Omar, and his wife. Omar loaned him his car so he could take Clara somewhere.

The road was quiet; there weren't too many cars around and the day was warm and sunny. Daniel and Clara drove along the Pan-American Highway to the northern part of Buenos Aires. A few days earlier, when they were in Mar de las Pampas, Clara made Daniel promise that he would take her to a special place. When he promised he would, she told him where she wanted to go. Now it was time to deliver on that promise.

On their drive, there was no sense of having to return. Daniel was driving calmly as they enjoyed the scenery that the lands of his country offered. In Argentina, as soon as you enter the highway you can see an expanse of green fields with soy, corn, and vegetables, and seeing a field full of sunflowers is an imposing scene.

Apart from really enjoying the view, they both felt that time spent together was special. They loved each other so much that stopping at a roadside stand just to get a sandwich was somehow special for them. Clara made him promise that he would take her to San Nicolàs to see the statue of the Virgin. Yes, after seventeen years without seeing each other, being together only for fifteen days on his first trip, and now after another eight months apart, she proposed making the 200-mile trip to go see the Virgin. It didn't sound very tempting or romantic to him, but he agreed anyway. It was really her Clara who was taking Daniel, and he knew it. Clara wanted to go there with him so she could ask the miraculous Virgin to take away his suffering and pain and to help him get cured.

She loved him deeply, and nothing was going to stop her from giving all of her love to Daniel. So, they drove those almost 300 kilometres and got there around 2 o' clock in the afternoon.

San Nicolás city, as in many other places, was where the Virgin decided to show herself and reveal her message to mankind.

On September 25, 1983, a humble native lady named Gladys noticed that the rosary that was hanging from her wall started shining in a rather strange way every time she was about to pray. She called her neighbors and none of them could find an answer to what was happening. From that moment on, Gladys kept on receiving messages from the Virgin in her house. Gladys decided not to say anything about it, so people wouldn't think she was crazy.

Clara didn't know the full story about this, but she had heard a lot about that Virgin and her miracles. People had deep faith in her, and many believed she was just like the Virgin that made her appearances in Fatima, Portugal in 1917, or the one in Lourdes, France, in 1858. Lots of people said that they saw the moment in which the sun started running in circles in the sky and came closer to the land, providing an indescribable sensation of light and peace.

Her message would be given later on.

Gladys had received many messages. Most of them talked about love, and the Virgin asked her to transmit her message to the world.

Gladys had told the priest that the Holy Lady wanted us to fill people's hearts with love.

In fact, every Virgin that showed up in different places and times was actually the same one: Holy Virgin Mary, mother of Jesus. She appeared in various places with a different name. Due to her faith, Clara was certain that it would be really good for Daniel to go there. That was why both of them were there, the reason they spent one day of the few they had together to go to visit the statue. How much would it be to travel almost 300 kilometres after having travelled over 17.000 ?

Gladys's decision not to tell anybody about her secret had a time sentence, since she had to tell Father Carlos. The priest suggested not spreading the news. Every message from the Virgin up to then had been silent.

The Virgin appeared in San Nicolás for seven years, and many families saw their rosaries glowing in their houses. They said they shone in a beautiful way and emitted sparkles that looked like tiny bolts of lightning.

Nobody had a scientific explanation for that event.

One day—prompted by what the Virgin had told her in one of her messages—Gladys wanted to see a picture of her. So she went to church and told the priest what was going on. He showed her a bunch of pictures, but Gladys didn't recognize the Virgin she had seen in her appearances.

Suddenly, Father Carlos realized he had forgotten that some old and abandoned pictures had been left in the bell tower. They went there together and when Gladys saw the pictures, she pointed at one of them and said that *that* was the Virgin she had been seeing in the messages.

Before her eyes was the image of Mary of the Rosary who arrived in San Nicolás in 1884, sent from Rome and blessed by Pope Leo XIII.

The picture had been placed in that church on September 25 1884, one hundred years earlier.

People say there is miraculous water in that place, but Clara and Daniel couldn't visit the fountain that day. Maybe they were meant to come back one day. Gladys had had dreams about a natural spring of water that emerged from a bush.

Five years later, Gladys had another dream about water; this time it ran from different canals surrounding the temple. In the dream, the Virgin showed Gladys the land where the temple and the bush were. A mysterious scent of roses surrounded the place, and when the land was dug up, crystalline water appeared at

154 feet. All of that happened in front of a priest, a geologist, and two architects. The water was taken in containers and many people experienced miraculous recoveries from it.

Nowadays, Gladys remains inside her house in San Nicolás de los Arroyos, Argentina. She continues to have discretion, as Father Carlos had suggested years before. Nobody knows if she still receives messages from the Virgin.

Clara had heard on other occasions that Argentina was somehow a special place in the world. It had definitely been a place of shelter for many Europeans during World War I and World War II.

Her Nonna (grandmother) had told her a little bit about the war. She really didn't want to talk about it as the memories were too painful. Besides, why would she tell her granddaughter sad things?

Clara saw pictures showing the poor conditions in which her grandmother and her brothers had lived. In one photo, they were standing very close together next to a broken wall, their little faces showing not even a hint of a smile. Silence was reflected in their sweet faces. For Clara's grandmother, Argentina had been shelter from deep and unimaginable pain, as it had for many other immigrants.

The Virgin had more messages for Gladys. In them, she asked for prayer. She told her that young people needed help, as drugs were invading the world and were capturing young souls. Young people were suffering from this threat. Gladys communicated that the Virgin wanted this message to be spread around the universe.

The Holy Virgin was telling everyone—not only Argentine people—that men had to reconsider their actions, that we needed *love*.

Clara thought, *Roles change when the most humble becomes the wisest because he learns to listen. And the wisest becomes the most ignorant and stubborn when his earlier eloquence vanishes, tormented by the things he cannot explain.*

Daniel and Clara waited in line together to see the Virgin's statue. Silently and holding hands, they found themselves in front of the statue that was kept safe inside a crystal box. The statue was of the Virgin carrying baby Jesus, and hanging from her hands was the rosary that had belonged to Gladys. Standing in front of the statue, Daniel took Clara by her waist and she touched his shoulder with her left hand. Daniel reached for the crystal with his right hand, trying to connect the Virgin with him; he had travelled all the way from Stockholm to Argentina and wanted to feel a connection with the Virgin. A few seconds went by like this—Clara and Daniel hugging. In the car on the way back to Buenos Aires, Daniel told Clara that he didn't feel that constant pain that had been with him for hours.

Daniel went back to Europe a few days later. So many things had happened in their lives, things that they could have never guessed were going to take place.

Undoubtedly ... men need to listen.

Undoubtedly ... the world needs *love*.

Don't you tell me ...

Don't anybody tell me they don't need love.

Don't let that man ... the big entrepreneur, successful and full of money, tell me that he doesn't need love.

Don't let that surgeon, with responsibilities and stress, admired or accused, tell me that he doesn't need love.

Let that baker from the corner store, the president of any country, the most famous movie star, that person that jumps from relationship to relationship trying to find something they haven't found yet—or maybe they did—come and tell me.

Let that poor beggar, who in the eyes of everybody else ironically seems to only need his own body and the clothes he has on to survive, come and tell me he doesn't need love.

Let the psychologist, the sexologist, the teacher, the mother, that sick person in a hospital, a professor, a mechanic, the pilot of the most modern of jets, a healthy one, a sailor, a priest, a rabbi, or an astronaut tell me that they don't need it.

Let's say that a hungry kid from Africa doesn't need love. Who could do it? He can't say it because hunger covers his mouth and he can't speak. His eyes cannot talk and his hands are unable to spread out to ask for something, just like a Hindu kid does.

His arms hang off the side of his body.

His hands don't spread out. It is an overwhelming sign of resignation.

Don't you tell me that the world doesn't need love.

Do we dare change what we say?

Can we stop procrastinating and do something to stop this from happening?

Let's start by saying all together:

Yes, the world does need love.

Chapter 8

Premonition

Clara was at home, watching a special about the Ice Hotel in Sweden. She felt attracted by the subject. This wonderful hotel was situated to the north of Sweden in Yukasjarvi, a small town of about seven hundred inhabitants on the banks of the Torne River. This river was said to be the most transparent river in the world. Eight hundred dogs lived in the town as well, for their inhabitants needed them for the sledges.

Suddenly the telephone rang. It was Daniel calling her from Sweden.

"Hello?" said Clara, who was still concentrating on what she had been attentively watching.

"Hello, beautiful," said Daniel through the receiver.

"Hello, my love! How are you?" said Clara in surprise.

"I'm very well. How is the nicest woman in the world?" asked Daniel.

"Completely fallen in love," she answered, smiling.

"Well ... and who is the lucky one?" asked Daniel.

"A black Viking ... ha ha. Have you ever seen a black Viking?" asked Clara.

"I swear that in almost eighteen years that I have been living in this country," said Daniel, "I have never seen one like that! Not even a dark- haired one."

Daniel was of Swiss ancestry, with white skin and dark hair. Under his thick eyebrows, his deep green eyes were full of expression. Those were the eyes that trapped Clara when he looked at her deeply, when they spoke to her, and when they looked at each other when he made love to her.

"You are adorable. I like you so much! Tell me, what were you doing?" Clara asked, wanting to know.

"Well, look! As I never think about a woman called Clara, who is in Argentina, I said to myself, *I will call her just to know if she feels like talking to a black Viking*," said Daniel.

"Of course. Why wouldn't I talk to the sexiest man in the world?" she said.

"Listen! Just now I have been for a little while in Argentina. I was talking to Omar," added Daniel anxiously.

"Don't you tell me, I have recently been to Sweden," said Clara.

"Ah! Yes! How about that?" Daniel said.

"I was watching a television special from Sweden which was showing the building of the ice hotel. It was really fascinating!" Clara told him.

"Well, it seems we were almost encountering or, better say, we were together as usual," said Daniel.

"Yes! It's true. We are one with the other. And what did Omar tell you, my love?" Clara asked, curious.

"We were talking about a job, about the possibility of getting something in Buenos Aires with him and even studying too," Daniel explained.

"That's great, my love! I wish you could get it. I know it's very difficult for you to make such an important decision. But you know that you can count on me," Clara told him.

"Yes, I know it, honey. It makes me feel so well to count on you," Daniel said.

"I want you to know," continued Clara, "that I am aware that what has happened is very hard for both of us. Mainly, because we are physically so far away from each other now. I know that it is harder for you to make the decision of coming here. But at the same time, we were so close, even though we were separated by thousands of miles of ocean. And our relationship is stronger and stronger … our love must be real. Don't you think so?" asked Clara.

"You shouldn't have the slightest doubt about it. The love I feel for you is the truest one that exists, beauty!" Daniel said.

"Yes, I know it. I am sure you must feel the same when I tell you how much I love you," said Clara. "You will see that everything will be solved little by little. Now everything is shocking, and besides—as we are the ones who can repeat that famous saying: *one never knows what life will bring about*—we don't know if what today seems difficult, later on turns into a possibility of growth, of movement, of being here and then there. We don't know what is going to happen. If we both want it, we will find a way. The oceans will separate and the distance will shorten, just like when time vanished when we met at San Martin and Maipú Avenues. Do you remember?" Clara said.

"Of course I remember," Daniel answered. "It was as if, in a minute, a curtain had gone down and years had been erased. It was as if there had been no distance or no time that would have separated us … Mmm … I'd love to kiss your lips right now," he murmured.

"I would love you to kiss me right now. You can't imagine how much I miss you … how much I miss your caresses," said Clara, recalling the moments shared together.

"And I can't tell you … I am mad. I can't wait any longer to have you with me in bed, to give you hundreds of kisses," added Daniel eagerly.

"My God! I die for being with you," said Clara in a soft voice.

Together, listening to each other, caressing the soul and the body, they continued talking as much as they could to calm down the thirst of love and their eagerness to be together. Sometimes, the fact that they couldn't meet and express their love felt like torture. But in a way, they felt so connected by their souls that their love became stronger day after day; it did not calm down or decay. And there was even more, as each night they shared their love with each other, giving each other the love that they had put off for so many years.

Sometimes, they spent one and a half hours talking on the telephone. Sometimes they spent more hours chatting on messenger. This kept them close together. But the pain of the separation—the fact that they couldn't see each other—was very hard for both of them. What they liked best was to talk on the phone, because this way they felt closer to one another. Listening to each other's voices so close in their ears gave them the sensation of being together in the same place. Many times, Clara cried for his absence; she felt the pain of not having him with her physically and not being able to speak face-to-face. Not being able to look at each other was so difficult. Looking into each other's eyes had always been a balm for both of them.

Meanwhile, as they were talking, Clara could catch a glimpse of the television screen. The place was almost magical, and the moonlight had a very special brightness. People who went there to help build the Ice Hotel came from all over the world. They said that the light in that natural environment was indescribably beautiful.

Inside the hotel, once the structure of the corridors and the rooms was built, the artists molded different sculptures of ice inside each room. They gave them a touch of magnificence that was reminiscent of a modern art gallery, but with the special distinction of the environment. One of the rooms had a furry reindeer cover. It was dark and it contrasted with the transparency of the place. Behind the bed were enormous snowballs of different sizes. Sometimes they seemed to detach from the wall and move; they were illuminated by fiber-optic lights that spread soft rays around the ambience releasing exquisite color tones.

They submerged themselves in each other as they gazed deeply into each other's eyes. The sensation of sailing the other person's soul by looking into their eyes was something they would never forget—something that they could have experienced in previous lives. It was something magic and transforming that they could transfer to sex.

Soon after, she recovered and continued thinking about what they both wished. At times, they would tell each other the same thing; they would talk about how they let time go by doing lots of activities to speed up time and that a new opportunity to meet was about to come.

One day, Daniel explained to her what winter was like there. It is not easy to imagine days of only three or four hours of daylight and then to see the night fall at 4 o'clock in the afternoon. The cold, which paradoxically seemed to burn your body; the snow at the entrance of the house preventing its lodger to exit; the cars covered in ice and snow.

"You cannot imagine how difficult it was for me to adapt to the northern cold," Daniel told her on the phone the following day.

"Yes, I guess it must have been hard, at least comparing it to Buenos Aires," confirmed Clara.

"Imagine, every day I had to get up early to clean the car and get it ready to start it. The previous night, I had to put a liquid into it to prevent the water inside the radiator from getting frozen and I also had to install a kind of heater inside the car so that in the morning, it wouldn't be so cold. It is really difficult to move your body with the amount of clothes you have to wear," said Daniel

And he continued:

"There are days and nights of about four degrees Fahrenheit below zero! I wished not even one coin fell onto the floor, because it is impossible to pick it up wearing so many thick layers of clothes and looking as sexy as the Michelin tire man."

"Ha ha!" laughed Clara. "You are sexy anyway, but ha ha!"

"In summer," said Daniel "days are warm and sunny. There are only four or five hours of darkness. It is especially beautiful. The environment is majestic," concluded Daniel.

Clara thought, *The charm of this magnificent place in the world surely consists of: The contrast between the gelid coldness and the arrival of hot weather; the deep and grey darkness of winter and the infiltrating, transparent, vital light of the warm season; the frightening, stormy skies and the soft, pinkish light of a magical, clear dusk in spring; the medieval culture and the technological advance; the legends of dark dragons and the blonde beauty of Swedish women.*

They ended their conversation. It was 11 p.m. in Buenos Aires. Daniel was tired and in bed. He put his cell phone on the night table. It was 4 a.m. in Sweden.

Clara and Daniel felt that their love was very strong.

They knew that the power of love could move mountains; it could make a person's life deeply change. True love didn't start in complete ecstasy, and that was what had happened to them.

Many times, events that take place in our lives do not allow us to consider the option that we deserve true love. Being loved—not for your possessions or your physical appearance, but because of what you hold *inside* in your soul—is a blessing. Why is it so difficult for us to consider ourselves as a *soul*? Yes, it is probably weird for some people to read this. But think deeply for a moment. Don't we see ourselves more as flesh, as a body, busy with the physical appearance, and worried about dressing according to fashion, instead of looking deep inside and considering our spiritual aspect? I mean, isn't it easier to consider ourselves as social actors immersed in a world that demands us to consume, to participate, or to follow a fashion in one way or another?

When we are able to stop and think about ourselves as body, mind, and spirit, we have a different perspective. It is not the same to look at your beloved one in the eyes and see his soul inside them. It is not the same to consider that person as a unit—made of those three aspects—instead of only looking at the body, separate from the rest. Allow yourself to be loved by that person, and consider that you deserve this kind of love. Give back to your love with your body and soul, without manipulations, with complete surrender.

Take a step backward and let your soul leave your body.

Now, look at it. What can you see? All that you have done up to now? Look at it again and observe what you are going to do from now on. Take a step forward and get into your soul again.

Do not stop; follow your destiny.

Clara recalled that summer afternoon when she was on holiday in Uruguay. She was staying in a cottage at a resort opposite the beach. From the cottage she could see a forest of high pine trees moving softly sideways in the wind. A breakfast under the pine trees was the starting point of a day full of nature and pure air. Very close to the cottage was a swimming pool surrounded by old trees and a very well-kept garden full of colorful flowers. At night, white smoke flowed from the chimneys of the grills of each cottage, a sign that their occupants had decided to cook a delicious barbecue at home. The smell of burning logs penetrated the nocturnal shadows that glittered against the light of the moon, letting her appreciate the golden and copper sparks of the flickering fire. What a nice Argentinian tradition it was to prepare a barbecue with friends in the open air! It was a pleasure to enjoy the long conversations, the anecdotes, the taste of the most delicious meat in the world with a wine brought from the best Argentine wine cellars, in this case shared with Uruguayan friends.

One morning, Clara woke up early and had breakfast in the open air at a small table, listening to the birds singing. It was a warm day and she decided to go to the swimming pool. She sat in the sun while she was reading a book, and then had lunch with her daughter and her family. In the afternoon, the weather started to change. Her daughter went to the cottage with her cousins. After sharing some coffee with her parents, her brother-in-law, and her sister, Clara went walking on a path that led to the beach.

The afternoon had become a bit tempestuous, so she put on the sweater she had on her shoulders. She walked along a dark wooden deck that took her to the beach via wide winding stairs. She stepped on the white sand. The sea was a bit wild and there was a fresh and constant wind that did not bother her. On the contrary, she enjoyed the touch of the wind on her face, leaving a few salty drops from the sea. She could see a boy in the water surfing over the agitated waves. The beach was deserted.

Clara sat on the sand and contemplated the sea. From time to time, somebody walked by. The bending coast seemed endless along both ends of the deserted beach. She continued looking at the sea and sometimes laid on her back on the sand and gazed up at the sky.

Pure white clouds were in turmoil. They moved along the sky very quickly. The sound of the breeze was imperceptible compared to the loud notes from the sea foam flooding the coast. Clara thought, *There are many reasons to be happy in my life, but something is missing … something that has to do with what completes a person. Certainly, it is about love, the one I have not yet found.*

Or the one she had lost. But at that moment she didn't know it.

Later on, she would remember—when she could put two and two together relating what she had felt that day lying on the sand next to the sea. As Clara stared at the sea, she wondered what was on the other side of the ocean. She would only remember that during her two hours alone that afternoon sitting opposite the ocean looking at the horizon, something attracted her in such a powerful way that made her keep thinking about the other side of the sea. What was there beyond the horizon? It was like a premonition, but she didn't have the slightest idea what would soon happen.

As she was looking far beyond, she felt a strong attraction arousing a strange curiosity inside her. Why was she wondering what there was behind that distant horizon? It was something she could not explain but that would be kept recorded in her memory forever.

It was twenty days later that Clara was at home with Estela and found Daniel's letter.

Chapter 9

Boundaries

Liquid, dense, clear ...

It started falling slowly down the cheekbone curve to its limit, where it acquired some speed, rapidly reaching the corner of the mouth. Tears taste salty.

Clara felt a tear rolling down her cheek until it touched her lips, but she didn't remove it. It was as though the deep pain and sadness took so much out of her that she didn't even have the strength to move or wipe away her tears.

As she sat in the dining room at home she wondered, *What am I doing here so lonely? What is he doing there so lonely? Would he be alone? Would he have gotten married? Was he tempted?*

His frequent calls and the way he pampered her didn't suggest that. He called her every night and they talked for two hours or more.

In the age of deception, double faces, and an extreme individualism that praised ego and lacked concern for other people, it was easy to think that he could be looking for comfort in the arms of another woman. On the other hand, it was unfair to think that he could deceive her when she was living the same situation—but below the equator—and *she* wasn't seeking comfort from someone else.

They were both strong and they trusted each other, but they sometimes had their doubts—as would any mortal in an unexpected situation like this one. On the other hand, it wasn't so surprising in our modern global world. There had to be many couples living a great distance apart, but it was the first time for them and they were living the experience holding on to the love that supported them day after day—a love that hadn't left them. Who knew why there had been so many years of pain ... why hadn't she been able to enjoy her life with another person?

She knew after so many years that it had been due to the loss of the loves of their lives: each other. She knew that now a door was opening before them. She was certain of that.

Meanwhile, Daniel was thinking exactly the same in Sweden. The telephone rang at Clara's house.

"Hello, beauty," Daniel said from the other side of the world.

"Hello, dear. What a nice surprise! I was just thinking of you," said Clara.

"I have called you, sweetheart, to tell you something I was just thinking of," said Daniel.

"Aha ..." answered Clara. "Tell me, please."

"I was thinking about us and what happened in our lives," said Daniel. "Why are we physically separated? Why was it that I had to follow my brother here to Sweden? On the one hand, I have to be thankful for having had the opportunity to live in such an organized society. I must be thankful for many things this country has given me. But then I go back to the time when I arrived here, and I think ... I've spent so many years building a relationship with the wrong person. Traveling with another woman when I should have been with you; changing a naturally perfect relation for a tasteless routine lacking pleasure, plagued with motionless. They are two different lives." He continued, "When I think of Argentina everything is warmer, hotter, human, it's as the human part of oneself. Do you understand me?"

"Yes, it's like roots," Clara agreed.

"It is as if, after such a long time, you aren't 100 percent Argentinian anymore," he told her.

"Yes sure, almost twenty years. It's logical to believe that time of your life is already a part of you," said Clara.

"But at the same time, if I think about it, I am not even 30 percent Swedish," Daniel said.

Clara was listening to him on the phone with the air-conditioning on because it was extremely hot in Buenos Aires that night, almost unbearable. On the other side of the world he was in bed, covered up to his chin. Outside, the excessive Swedish wind was blowing in the rigorous winter. "It wasn't so cold," Daniel had told her.

"Only 20 degrees below 0". "Here in Sweden," Daniel said, "in spite of you being a good, honest and responsible person and doing your job well, they always remind you that you are good but, you are a foreigner. For instance, you go to work every day and Swedish people have the capacity to walk by your side and study you. They would be excellent poker players. They would never tell you if you were doing something wrong or unexpected. They only observe you and maybe they tell you something after a long period of time. In Argentina it was totally different. I remember that if your boss looked at you or had something to tell you he did it and he didn't pretend in the process," continued Daniel.

"That must have been one of the things which are part of the difficult task of adapting oneself to another culture, because it is simply different from ours, isn't it?" added Clara.

"Certainly," replied Daniel.

Clara was listening to him and the story reminded her of her readings of Edward Hall's books when she was at university. These readings described the different concepts of time in different places—concepts of time in American native tribes and in Latin working environments, where time and the way people behaved regarding time were not understood by certain people. Culture also differs in the Middle East, where time, meetings, and people's attitudes about those meetings could seem completely absurd for anybody in the western side of the world, like an American or a Swede.

"Sometimes you don't understand their humor," continued Daniel, "like what they are laughing at. All that time, not months but *years*, the experiences you live don't have the same feeling. I remember once when I lived in Argentina I took a packet of cigarettes and I asked people around me if they wanted one, just for kindness. Everybody wanted one. Or sometimes if somebody was smoking with a group of friends and you didn't have a cigarette at that moment, you asked for one and they gave it to you with pleasure," Daniel explained.

And he went on talking.

"Well, one day I was at work here in Sweden and during break time, a guy asked me for a cigarette. I gave him one. But, he wanted to pay me for it! Do you understand?" said Daniel in amazement.

"Oh no, I can't believe it!" said Clara.

"Yes, he wanted to pay me for *a* cigarette. It was just as if ... as if he didn't want to owe me anything at all," added Daniel.

"Yes, of course. I understand. He asks you for it, but at the same time he wants to cancel the debt, *just in case this guy asks me for something more than what he gave to me*. It also happens here, maybe not as notorious. There are certain people who are afraid of receiving something because they don't want to give it back, even when the one who gave it to them doesn't expect anything in return," concluded Clara.

"It is something very similar, something of the kind. As if they didn't know how to give to others without having something in return," said Daniel. "Sometime later on, I was talking to another colleague about drinks," he continued. "*Which one do you like best, Coke or Fanta?*" I asked. After a while I went to get a can from the drinks machine. I bought something to drink for myself and I also bought another can and gave it to him. The guy looked at me in astonishment and suddenly asked: "Why?"

to which I replied, "I don't know, I just bought one for me and another one for you!" He stared at me and, after two hours or so, not more, he came back and gave me another can in return for the one I had given him. It was bizarre, as if he couldn't let the day go by without closing a debt with me, so that everything was clear," ended Daniel.

It's incredible how we human beings still have so much to learn! Although we are intelligent beings living on the planet earth, we haven't been able to notice so many things we must change in the world. If only could man realize that all lines are imaginary—that the Greenwich Meridian divides the East from the West only in people´s minds.

If only man could realize that the equator separates the northern hemisphere from the southern hemisphere and you can only see it drawn if you look at it on a map. That the west is not better or worse than the east, that Americans or Europeans are exactly the same as people from Africa, Asia, or any other part in the world. Everybody is really alike; our essence is alike.

If we could become aware that the west needs the wisdom of the east ... that maybe, one day, the northern hemisphere might need the southern hemisphere. That if we don't take care of our environment, our planet Earth, if we spoil natural resources wildly for the benefit of a few people, forgetting about the rest, we will end up worse than whatever we could imagine.

If only we realized that power, submission and domination in relationships, and ambition—these have led man to take away territories from the aborigines and to create imaginary lines now called borders.

If we could fly up and away from Earth, as an astronaut does, and watch it from outer space, we would see that those lines do not exist, that we have made them up. And that we definitely ended up building them, separating people and pulling them apart.

We are all a small piece of the universe. All our souls in our bodies are united, and in the net of interrelationships we establish among one another, we are all connected to such an extent that we can have an effect on others in spite of the distance. It doesn't matter where we are—in which place or at what time.

Undoubtedly, what we do or say has a certain effect on the rest of the world. That is how Daniel and Clara's lives had been affected by the convergence of space and time. Their lives were also affected by the decision of those who evaluated Daniel at work, those who had decided not to grant him the illness pension yet—preventing him from doing what he wanted and constricting his life. Those people were discussing the claim of an ill person, fixing evaluating meetings every three months with no solutions.

That is how, many times, the lives of one or more people hang by a thread under the decisions of someone else who might not know the consequences of those decisions on others. How can anybody believe that a person suffering from arthrosis and arthritis proven by medical professionals must remain tied to other people's decisions? Aren't having a chronic disease and suffering from constant pain enough punishment? Could it be that twenty years of devotion and work for a country doesn't earn one the right to at least be free of certain worries if one has to suffer from an illness? Should that be a consequence of having been born below the equator?

Is it possible to have fewer rights than another person because you were not born in the same country? Can a person be considered not to belong to a territory, delineated by invisible boundaries, even though that person has served and worked in that country for the benefit of its people?

Could an open-minded view from the doctors who examine you at work compensate for suffering physical pain when you are ill? Can they allow you the possibility of freely making your own decisions?

Daniel was eager to be with his beloved, the woman he had lost. Meaningful coincidences, what Deepak Chopra calls *synchrodestiny* had made her suddenly appear in his path again. If only he could have the freedom to decide when to go to Argentina and come back to Sweden! If only he could be next to Clara anywhere, if she could look after him and accompany him.

If only he could keep the bonds with that beautiful country, Sweden, and its people. If only he could be near his children forever. If only he could join everything he loved.

Clara and Daniel would have to see what would happen. They would have to see how they could help their *synchrodestiny*.

Maybe they didn't know it yet, but one way to help their *synchrodestiny* would be to have the feeling that they deserved their love. If they asked the universe that their dreams of living in Argentina and Sweden would come true, those dreams would become real no matter how difficult they seemed to be.

They had to relax and trust that—in the same way that Daniel's presence had appeared in her life and Clara's presence had suddenly come into his life—the miracle would take place. They only had to be alert to the signs, to relax, and to feel confident.

Chapter 10

Not Believing

Almost a year had gone by since Daniel's second visit. Every plan they made to be together had to be postponed a bit, since he was putting a lot of effort into changing certain situations related to his job and his illness. He also thought that even though his eldest boy was already at university, the two youngest were still adolescents and they needed his father's presence.

According to what he had told Clara, Daniel felt he should have thought about divorcing the first time he had separated from his wife years before. Between work and his illness, he couldn't catch a break economically speaking, so even planning a trip somewhere was not possible. Clara and Daniel were both sure that they wanted to do the best they could—but *together*.

It was not possible for Clara to collect money to travel because she did not earn much as a teacher. She depended on the person who had hired her to work in that company. Moreover, she was alone with her children and she had to afford living in a big house, which was supposed to be maintained by a man with a high-paying job—someone earning at least five times what she earned as a teacher. She did not receive any help for her children. So, she had to pay for the school, clothes, and whatever they needed.

Clara was a down-to-earth person. She could have asked Daniel or insisted on him collecting money to pay for a ticket for her to go to Sweden. She was eager to go there and discover the gorgeous country. But she thought Daniel deserved to come back to his land, as he had so many friends and relatives he had stayed in touch with but could not see. He needed to come to his country to be able to evaluate living again in Argentina one day. If he left Sweden, he was going to lose everything he had built there; Clara knew it was not an easy decision to make. Daniel had to make sure he would earn enough money to be able to come and go as he pleased, the same way it had to be for Clara.

- Place: Buenos Aires, Argentina.
- Time: 2007

Buenos Aires is hot in January. Somebody coming from Stockholm had a letter for Clara. It was Daniel's brother. She waited patiently for his call. When he landed at Ezeiza airport, he called Clara and promised her that he would give her the letter during the course of that week. He called her once more and little by little started telling her about his impression of the country, which was bad, he felt, compared to Sweden's comfort and safety.

This attitude surprised Clara, since she had heard foreigners talk wonders about Argentina. In fact, she had read interviews in the newspaper in English, French, Dutch and several other languages by people who declared to be in love with this land and even wanted to live here. The most ironic thing was that the person saying this was Argentine!

According to his perspective—which wasn't always wrong—all the bus driving was a disaster; buses went from one lane to the other shaking everybody standing inside them. They had to struggle and fight against the tireless force of physics that duplicated—actually, multiplied—itself when they had to make a turn. Traffic seemed more like a herd of buffalo on the

American steppe than a tidy and organized line of cars on a highway, the product of a good driving education.

And yes, thought Clara. *He was right in a way. We should be able to educate our people to get better results. It's never too late.*

The dialogue continued—or rather the monologue did—describing mosquitoes as war jets throwing bombs into foreign territory until every place free of blankets was devastated. It is perfectly understandable to not be used to mosquitoes when you come from the cold north. Ironically, Clara would learn later on that you can find plagues of mosquitoes in Sweden too, close to the lakes—in spite of the cold. Plus, he added, the view of poor people going through the trash made him think, *this is Cambodia.*

This last remark made Clara feel bad and she thought that George's and Daniel's next meeting in Sweden would probably not encourage Daniel to come back to Argentina after all that negativity. His opinions surely weren't going to help Clara and Daniel. Besides, Clara loved her country and knew that Argentina, thank God, was very, very far from being like Cambodia. No offense to any Cambodian who was a victim of one of the most violent regimes of the twentieth century. Actually, there's no register on how many people were exploited, tortured, and killed in the so-called *death fields* in Cambodia. Without doubt, they were two very different realities.

Something was clear to Clara: when we talk we have to know that words have value and meaning, and sometimes we have to watch what we say.

Suddenly, the conversation took a different road, and without knowing how it happened, Clara heard George saying:

"If I came back to Argentina ... imagine! I wouldn't leave my own children. I have a boy and a girl. They are a bit younger than my brother's. Some people may say they are big enough, but they aren't! They are sixteen and thirteen years old. It's like telling you to leave your kids," George exclaimed on the phone.

You didn't have to be that smart to get the underlying—or actually pretty direct—message that was being sent. Clara thought that hadn´t happened to him, but it did happen to Daniel. Life had given Daniel a second chance. Life was actually giving both of them, Clara and Daniel, that second chance.

The idea of being apart from the kids for a few months was on Daniel's mind. What George didn't know was that Clara had never asked Daniel to be separated from his children. Clara loved Daniel, and when you really love someone you want what's best for that person. You want him or her to be happy. You want to see that person smile and enjoy life with people he or she loves as well.

Clara knew that the love she felt for Daniel included knowing she wasn't the only person he loved. She knew how much he loved his children; both Daniel and Clara wanted to find a way to combine everything so that everybody was happy. Of course that included the idea that Daniel had never asked her to leave her own children either—the same way Clara had never thought of leaving them.

Clara thought that George, who wanted the best for Daniel, most probably found it difficult to imagine Clara—a tall, voluptuous, and sexy woman—as a good person. Without knowing her, it was easier to think that she was with Daniel for some kind of personal gain. She knew, by experience, that the image is the first thing you see in a person.

People often make interpretations that lead them to draw conclusions based on those interpretations. Therefore, they can develop wrong concepts about how a person is deep inside.

Clara was modest when it came to clothes. She rarely wore a low neckline, but her face and presence made heads turn when she walked into a room. She had sex appeal. That is something you can't get with surgery, collagen, or liposuction. It was something inside her. And at the same time, inside her, lived a noble and honest person with strong convictions.

George was making wrong conclusions. He didn't believe Clara and was suspicious of her. But Clara was completely faithful to Daniel. She wasn't afraid to admit it, even in a world full of deceit where lying to another person is appreciated in order to be *number one* when it comes to one-night stands, affairs, and more.

Daniel and Clara knew how they managed to have a long distance relationship, and Clara wasn't planning to explain her intimacy with Daniel to anybody. Of course it was very likely that after a year apart, people considered cheating, but these people hadn't gone through what they had.

As a very young girl, Clara had gone through the experience of helping witnesses of tragedies, trying by any means to alleviate their pain. For years, she had to deal with the psychological consequence that this brought about to those people. Daniel had experienced difficult moments as well.

Nobody knows what it's like to go through hard times unless you experience them yourself. Even so, there are some people who learn nothing from those experiences. In spite of that, we are all capable of resilience that makes us stronger after a complicated and difficult situation. This is just like in the world of physics, when matter recovers its initial form after being altered. Nobody knew what Clara and Daniel felt, the trust and respect that existed between them. Every experience they had in their lives had had an effect on their minds and taught them to go on no matter what happened. In a way, they both felt they had accomplished something by dedicating themselves to former couples and giving more and more, he to his wife and she to her husband—even though they weren't the ones destined for them.

Clara hated lying and she wasn't going to do anything to hurt the love of her life, especially after thinking she'd lost him and given him up forever—especially, after having found him again. Only she knew what had happened that day two years before, when she found the letter Daniel had left her before going to Europe.

They felt a phase in their lives had passed. Now another one was starting, one in which of course their children would be involved. Nobody could understand or give their opinion about something they didn't experience, about something that hadn't happened to them. Clara knew how deeply she loved Daniel and she wanted the best for him, especially now that he was sick and she felt the necessity of helping him—tearing her up.

She wanted to be by his side and give him the love he deserved as a person and as her man. Then she heard—and she even understood—other people's opinions, but she couldn't help feeling bitter after their comments. Clara decided to forgive every unfounded suspicion because she knew that George's intention was to protect Daniel.

Clara had also heard people she barely knew say that Daniel was going to cheat on her, that he was using her by having fun traveling every now and then to have an affair with her. She also heard them saying that this was a virtual love. She controlled her urge to answer rudely and thought that maybe it was best to let some time go by and let time speak for itself.

Some people need to be reminded that words like *loyalty* and *trust* still exist.

Not believing can lead us to make wrong decisions. Being capable of trusting can open doors that are unimaginable for us. Clara and Daniel *believed*. They knew they were going to be together one day. They were certain of it.

Clara thought, *If we could make time and space converge so that our bodies could be together. I say bodies because our souls are already together, they've always been. That is why other people can't understand how we hold each other in a long distance relationship. I actually think it is because we both belong to another dimension that isn't regulated by postmodern concepts, and we don't need to prove anything to ourselves or others. It is a concept that comes with knowing to value things that happen to you in life, even if they are bad and can cause such pain that penetrates you like a drill at full speed. Even though they bring pain, they happen in order to give us the chance to learn to value the good things.*

When you do that, nothing gets you off the road leading to more good things. When this goes on in your life, and you can taste it, touch it and savor it ... you don't want to lose it for anything in the world.

Daniel had told Clara on the phone about his experience of people giving advice to him in Sweden.

One night he phoned her and said,

"You know what beauty? Some days ago I was at work and a friend came to buy something for his motorbike. We ended up talking about life. As he knew about our story because I had told him about us and how we met again he asked me ... 'And you are calmed?'" He was referring to the question his friend had asked him.

"'Yes, of course,' I answered," said Daniel.

"But how can you know that she isn't with another guy? It's been too long,' my friend added," commented Daniel.

"It's just that, it is not the time or place that gives you this serenity. There are couples that live together and live separate lives and cheat on each other almost every day," explained Daniel to Clara while referring to the conversation with his friend.

"Imagine being this far, then!" commented Daniel's friend.

"It's ... you can't understand it, only Clara and I know," Daniel said, repeating to Clara what he had told his friend.

Clara listened attentively to Daniel. She told him she could understand perfectly well what he was talking about. After that, she told him what she had heard once when her cousin asked her something.

"So, when is he coming?" Kathy had asked her.

"He can't make it right now," answered Clara in a calm tone of voice. "He is getting some things together."

"Well, I believe you should sort out some kind of arrangement in which you guys are allowed to live your lives until you meet again," added Kathy.

It was clear that they were talking to her about sex, right? Clara thought, *And who has asked for your opinion?* Another person's opinion was similar to Kathy's.

"And what are you going to do? This seems like a platonic relationship to me!" Clara thought, *It can seem whatever you want to you, the important thing is what it means to Daniel and me.*

Once more Clara found herself thinking, *I never asked what this looked like to you.* She repeated her thought to Daniel on the phone.

Maybe we should ask those people how much money they have in their bank accounts. How much do they spend every month? These are simple questions that most people wouldn't want to answer, right? They'd probably be beating around the bush before answering something like that. Still, they felt they had the right to talk about Clara and Daniel's life just because something remarkable had happened to them.

Daniel said,

"I think that nobody other than us can realize what we feel. What I felt with you, the love, your ways, and everything you gave me, I felt it with you, and there isn't another Clara in this world."

"Yes, love, I know," Clara replied. "Everything that happened to me the day I found your letter, the feeling that went over my body and soul and that following sensation of something pushing me to find you. Nobody can understand it without living it."

"I love you, beautiful," murmured Daniel in her ear from the northern hemisphere. I love you too," said Clara.

"You give me so much, honey ... that by only talking to you my soul is full. I feel complete. I don't desire another woman," Daniel told her.

"You should know that by only being next to you, when we were sitting at the table, for example, and talking, it made me experience an indescribable feeling of happiness. Just to have you next to me. It's like your being completes mine in a way that makes me feel fulfilled and entranced, yet conscious at the same time. I wouldn't allow another man to even touch my shoulder with the tip of his finger. I wouldn't do anything to hurt you. I love you, Daniel," said Clara.

"I adore you, love. Let's talk tomorrow. You don't know how well it makes me feel when I talk to you," he said.

"Yes, my God, call me tomorrow, I will be waiting for your call," murmured Clara in a soft sexy tone.

"Of course. Good night, beautiful."

"Until tomorrow, baby. Have a good night's rest," said Clara.

> In times like these: globalized, contradictory, where everybody communicates with everybody, where individualism triumphs over everything, we come first only if it's good *for me*. Only if *I* want to, if there are benefits for *me*.
>
> In these times, the other person doesn't exist—or only exists if he can do something for me. In this day and age, companies keep moving and everything is constantly changing. It is a throwaway culture where everything renews itself.
>
> Nowadays, human relations absorb these kinds of conditions and people think it is okay being with somebody. If someone else comes along, why not?
>
> In this way, people own a particular perspective related to the performer's subjectivity. Today I am with you, but tomorrow I don't know; only

> if it's good for me. If something better doesn´t come along.
>
> This way, many women have tried to have the same rights men have historically had since the dawn of time. They assume this attitude—pretending to be independent, acting like trophy collectors, and not realizing that this attitude really hurts them. The reason is that people who act like this, haven't got their souls fulfilled, since we all need love, regardless of our gender.
>
> This can probably result in a constant search for love, because everybody is in the same situation. Passing from one person to another and this level of lies generates a sense of emptiness that rules everything. People lie to themselves.
>
> Finding that person who fills every corner of our body and soul is a blessing that many want to achieve.

Clara and Daniel had experienced it when they were forty. It had started with that first kiss, then with verbal communication, and the infiltration of the other one's soul through their eyes. And it reached the point when many signs emanated through every cell and fiber of their bodies, from north to south, covering every cardinal point of their bodies.

The following night, it was 2 a.m. in Sweden when Daniel called Clara. They had to arrange the phone calls because of the difference in time. Daniel was five hours ahead of Clara's time in Argentina. So he sometimes set the alarm clock at 2 a.m. to phone her at about 9 p.m. in Buenos Aires because, before this time, Clara was still working.

When Clara picked up the receiver he immediately started telling her another fantastic love story:

"The dragon and the tigress are on a beach that looks like paradise. The hotel they are staying at is located on a hill that allows them to see the blue seawater. The weather is hot, the evening is about to end, and the still heat expands in a warm hug that fills the room with a taste of unmistakable desire.

They decide to go for a walk. They are both barefoot, since the softness of the floor allows it. She is wearing a short dress over her bikini. He is wearing a swimsuit and a T-shirt. They walk through a track that leads to a path ahead. To move forward they need to make their way through some big soft leaves that appear on the narrow path.

He is holding her hand and the road goes downhill. You can see white sand from time to time. The cool breeze moves the vegetation that surrounds it. Down on the coast, they can see a small beach in a corner of the actual beach that is filled with tall rocks and vegetation.

When you go further down the road, the sound of the waves caressing the sand becomes clearer and inviting, suggestive.

They arrive at the place together and run to the shore, where they wet their feet in the foam and go into the sea a little bit further on. She lets him go and in a precise move she lifts her foot, splashes him with some water and smiles.

He immediately chases her and splashes her with salty seawater drops. Holding her by her waist he kisses her mouth, they caress each other, and they end up lying on the shore, wet by the foam that covers their bodies again and again, going along with the movement of their love, playing with their sensations and perceptions."

Chapter 11

Orbiting the Earth

Daniel had at last gotten the money for the trip. He was exhausted; he had done everything he could to reach his objective. Now he only had to arrange some details at his job and ask for permission to leave the country. They tried to stop him from traveling to check that the trip did not affect his health. They asked him to go to the doctor a couple of times due to his suffering from arthritis.

Sitting before his computer, he opened the e-mail box and read a message from Clara:

To: daniel@lovemail.com
From: clara@lovemail.com
Subject: When?

DANIEL- CAR- HIGHWAY- AIRPORT- ARLANDA- PLANE- OCEAN-BUENOS AIRES- AIRPORT- EZEIZA- CLARA- LOOKS- HUG- MORE HUGS- KISSES- TEARS- MORE KISSES- PARKING LOT- CAR- HIGHWAY- HOME- CORRIDOR- STAIRS- BEDROOM- LOVE ... When are you coming?

Clara
♥

Daniel read her e-mail. He was as anxious as she was for them to see each other, to be together again. And he answered as soon as he read it.

To: clara@lovemail.com
From: daniel@lovemail.com
Subject: RE: When?

CAR- HIGHWAY- PLANE- ARGENTINA- CLARA- DANIEL- LOOKS- HUG- KISSES- BAD WORDS- HANDS RUNNING OVER- CAR- HIGHWAY AGAIN- HOME- STAIRS- BEDROOM- DRAGON- TIGRESS- BED- LOVE- SIX HOURS- EIGHT HOURS- DAWN- THEY START AGAIN- MORE ... I arrive on Saturday morning on flight n° 863 Iberia. Are you coming for me? Get ready because you have no idea of what is awaiting you.

I LOVE YOU,
Yours always,
Daniel.
♥

After a year of separation they could at last be together again. Clara woke up early, took a shower, and got ready. She wore a beautiful black dress, high black boots, a touch of perfume, and a suede coat. She arrived at Ezeiza airport on time and had a coffee at a bar while she waited for his flight to arrive. More than forty-five minutes passed when she finally heard the announcement of the flight arriving from Barcelona, Spain. She still had to wait for the disembarking and customs.

Clara went close to the door where people carrying their suitcases were starting to arrive. The air was filled with anxiety. She was concentrating on the door and looked at the corridor that would lead Daniel back to her arms. She suddenly saw him. She looked at him directly but he could not see her among so many people cramped at the entrance. She walked toward the right where Daniel was coming out. Along the corridor some other people were walking beside him. They looked at each other for an instant doused with intensity as she walked toward him.

Thus, in the middle of the corridor, they met in a long hug followed by an endless kiss. They were in the middle of a crowd, obstructing the flow of people who had to dodge them in order to continue on their way.

For an instant, they lost the track of time until they came back to reality and moved aside. They were hugging and smiling and kept stopping to look at each other and pat their faces to reassure themselves that they were together.

And the eternal love scene was repeated when they arrived at the house. Time seemed to disappear and—unbelievable or not—they felt as if no time had gone by. They felt as if they had always been together, united by the magic of belonging to the same universe—that one we believed to be the only one until scientists proved otherwise. They were together, like microcrystal particles floating in the universe. Like chords emitting musical notes in a space that cannot be seen, but that kept them united.

That was the way they felt when they were physically next to each other. And they had felt that way all those years they had been physically separated. But they had been united like particles floating in the universe, which are capable of being in more than a place at the same time. This was exactly the way they had experienced—so many times—feeling the presence of each other, as if they were side by side. It was as though you could turn around and communicate with someone who was not physically there, but this person's soul was next to you—even though his or her body was physically in another place.

Daniel had experienced feeling her caressing him while he was sleeping. That had made him wake up suddenly, feeling this sensation on his skin, feeling her hand softly running along his back. He had even turned around to see if there was anybody there because it had felt *so real*!

What was astonishing to Daniel the day after that happened was that Clara wrote him an e-mail telling him that she had been daydreaming. In her dream, she was softly touching his back with her hand. When he checked what time she had written the email, he realized that it was exactly the time at night when he had been dreaming of her. He wondered, *Could it be that the power of thinking in one another was able to make her thoughts come true, in spite of the distance and the separation?*

She, on the other side of the world, read the e-mail Daniel had sent her telling her his dream—what he had felt on his skin during the night, how he suddenly woke up to check what was going on, and the weird sensation he felt due to that experience.

They had had such experiences.

Once, at the beginning, when Daniel had not come back to Argentina, he told her in an e-mail:

Yesterday I had a beautiful dream I was in Argentina and I met you on a street. I don't know, it was strange—you were walking along that street in Tigre. And I met you and we hugged for some long minutes and I kissed you. It was a beautiful dream, it was so real!

Clara checked her e-mail and read this. She couldn't believe her eyes! She was in a cyber café on a street in the community of Tigre! She had gone there to give a lecture, which was unusual for her; she had never before gone to work to Tigre. He had dreamed that they met on a street in Tigre, and finally they did. She was walking on a street when she suddenly felt an urge to check her e-mail. She went into that cyber café, checked her e-mail, and read his words in astonishment. They met via mail there! It was really amazing and still hard for them to believe. Were these kinds of events *signs* to show them something?

Clara and Daniel were in the room.

"Hello, pretty. Hi, beautiful. How much I missed you!" said Daniel.

"Hi, god of the universe ... you cannot imagine how much *I missed you*," Clara said.

"No, *I missed you more*," he said.

"Impossible," she replied.

Clara ran her fingers through his hair while she was talking to him, looking at him, swimming her thoughts inside his dilated pupils as if she were an ophthalmic solution trying to heal the physical separation evidenced in his eyes, a separation that no longer existed.

"What has happened in our lives? It's mad the way destiny joined us together again," said Daniel.

"Yes, it's destiny that gave us the correct signs, and we paid attention to them—we valued them. We did not let them pass by," affirmed Clara with certainty.

"Yes, beauty. It's true neither of us let this pass by," Daniel agreed.

"That is due to the love that unites us, because both of us know who we are and we want to be together," said Clara.

"Yes, I always think, *I was lucky that you kept my letter, and we were lucky that your friend told you.* How was it?" asked Daniel.

"I do not want to come next Saturday here and get to know that you haven't found out what his e-mail address is!" announced Clara, smiling. As she said this, she wagged her finger, imitating her friend when she encouraged her to write to Daniel that first time.

"Yes, and you also kept the letters I sent you from Mendoza more than twenty-five years ago," said Daniel.

"Aha, we have already celebrated our silver anniversary. Ha ha. You see? It was okay because we skipped the daily routine, the quarrels ..." said Clara.

"But hold on a second! Do not establish any expectations, because now I am going to throw some plates at you and beware of taking the remote control or watching football on TV!" Clara said, tickling him.

"No, no, please ... that I cannot ... ha, ha, ha! No! Now you'll see, you don't know what is going to happen to you!"

exclaimed Daniel in laughter. He held her by her arm and ... the telephone rang.

"I must answer!" murmured Clara while laughing.

"I'm going to think about it," he replied as he picked up the phone and gave it to her.

"Hello," said Clara.

"Hi! Is it Clara?" replied the voice on the other end of the phone.

"Yes, who is it?" she asked.

"It's me, Gerardo, Daniel's friend," said Gerardo.

"Hi, Gerardo. How are you?" said Clara, smiling.

"Fine. How are *you*? Happy to have the Abominable Snowman with you?" he said.

"Imagine, of course I am happy! Here he is, next to me, anxious to talk to you. Shall I get you through?" asked Clara.

"Okay, it was nice to talk to you Clara," said Gerardo.

"Bye, friend. We wait for you and your wife to share a barbecue together one of these days, kiss," said Clara.

"Thank you for the invitation! See you, a kiss to you!" said Gerardo.

Daniel and Gerardo remained talking on the phone. Clara left him alone to let him talk freely with his friend. She took a shower and changed clothes. Her hair was still wet. When she came back to the bedroom, he looked at her while he continued talking to his friend. He put down the phone and approached her from behind while she was tucking the blouse into her trousers in front of the mirror. He stood behind her and put his arms around her waist, kissed her neck, looked at her in the mirror, kissed her cheek, and whispered in her ear, "*I love you.*"

And Clara followed her routine because she couldn't do anything else; she kept on going to work every morning. He, meanwhile, used that time to visit friends and relatives. After that, they shared every minute together—the few hours left each day and some time alone after going out for dinner with some friends.

One night Daniel went to a meeting with his old school friends. They had dinner, talked about their lives, and Daniel told them how life had brought him and Clara together again. Many of them were really astonished and some of them met him again some days afterward.

Some days later, Clara and Daniel were invited for a barbecue at Omar and his wife's house—as well as to many other's houses or apartments. They also went to Clara's relatives' houses and Daniel's relatives in Martínez. She introduced him to her friends as well, sharing intense and amusing moments while having dinner.

Luciano, Clara's brother, talked with Daniel for a long time, asking him about Sweden and its people, their habits and routines. Sometimes Daniel was asked to say something in Swedish. Whoever listened to him would answer: "*Yes, sure*"—most probably not having the slightest idea of what he was saying. Clara had learned a few words like *Jag sakna dig* which means *I miss you*. Or the words she had read in the card he had sent her some months before that read:

Idag, Imorgon, För Evigt Jag tanker pä dig hela tiden!

Today, tomorrow, forever I think about you at any time.

They were so happy together! Moreover, both enjoyed the moments shared with friends: barbecues, homemade pasta, and good wine accompanied by long, interesting conversations. However, they heard some comments that were not pleasant. They came from people who were judging the situation.

Then Clara heard the following comment from the wife of one of Daniel's friends who lived nearby and had shared acquaintances: "Well, as we live so close to one another, it seems you will have to be careful!"

Clara thought about the irony of this. *What was she trying to say? That she cheats on her husband so she is afraid of me seeing her with someone else and spreading the news? Or in any case what she believes is that, as Daniel lives in Europe, I may go out with another man and consequently I will have to be careful that nobody sees me?*

It was clear that Patricia, Daniel's friend's wife, was accusing—or even saying she *believed*—that Clara was going to cheat on Daniel only because of the fact that they lived in different countries.

Of course, the situation was quite interesting, filled with emotion and strange coincidences that had united them in a very special way. This could lead people to be envious and make false conclusions.

This woman sounded suspicious of Clara. She was judging someone else's life and behavior without really knowing the person, based on a completely unfounded and unjustified accusation that was made up in her mind.

It was evident that she didn't know that Clara was with Daniel only because she loved him. And this woman was lucky enough to have a person beside her, someone to share her life with. Clara and Daniel had had to be separated. Daniel was going through an illness, taking strong medicine. Clara had not chosen to be with a man going through such pain and suffering only to end up lying to him or cheating on him. She wouldn't have done that even if he had been perfectly healthy. There was nothing else to say.

Someone else said this to her:

"And have you been with somebody else since you separated from your husband? Have you tried being with another man before being with Daniel?" This was asked of her by a man who was said to be Daniel's friend.

This was really a very personal question. When she met Daniel again she had already been living alone with her children for four years. Why should she explain something so private to the man that was asking the question? thought Clara.

"I mean, because you must live life … you must try," Fabio said.

The man who was talking seemed to be saying that Clara needed to have some other experiences before making a decision, or that perhaps someone else could give her something better. It was clear he was talking about sex. Somehow it sounded funny listening to someone who thought they knew everything about sex. In any case, all he knew was *his* way of having sex and *his* experiences. What he apparently did not know was that Clara and Daniel were united by a true, deep love and that this was not a love adventure for any of them.

"It was enough for me to be with the most masculine man in the world to make a decision," said Clara. "Besides, my children never met anyone. They would only meet a person I deeply loved, someone I knew would love them and respect them," answered Clara.

Daniel, meanwhile, got this question from someone.

"And, are you really separated?" his friend's wife wanted to know.

At this level, they felt they had to hear and ignore people prejudging them. This had happened to them in their lives and they knew how much they loved each other, how much they had to suffer for being separated by such a great distance.

They had been lucky enough to have met again. Nobody knew how it felt to recover the person you loved all of your life. Nobody knew how much they had thought about one another, in different situations, in strange moments, under the influence of weird premonitions.

This led Clara to remember something from long before, one or two years after Daniel had left. She had found herself inside a shop in a mall, staring motionless at a card she read and afterward bought and kept in the little box. The card had a beautiful picture and what was written on it seemed to speak to her.

May the road ...

... And until we meet again,

May God hold you in the palm of His hand.

(Old Irish prayer, author unknown)

Clara did not think about anything at that moment. She only read it, bought it, and kept it for a long time.

Once again, an airplane. Once again, a departure. And once again, the separation. This time it was harder than before. They pretended to be strong, hiding their pain.

Gerardo arrived at Clara's house to take Daniel to Ezeiza airport.

Daniel and Clara embraced in the kitchen, hiding the vulnerable feelings metabolizing in their bodies.

Yet, when they were hugging at the door before he got into the car, Daniel said:

"Bye, fool."

"Bye, stupid. I'm fed up with you!" said Clara, smiling.

Gerardo looked at them in surprise, astonished but smiling at the same time, because of the way they were handling the situation. They had their own codes, a special inside joke as a couple.

The departure time had arrived and Daniel was about to find himself orbiting the earth.

The car left and their souls were torn apart once again.

Chapter 12

The Letter Seventeen Years Later

Some days after Daniel's departure, Clara found the letter Daniel had given her before her wedding. And she wrote to him.

To Daniel: daniel@lovemail.com
From Clara: clara@lovemail.comm
Subject: The letter seventeen years later.

Dear Daniel, my love,

When you wrote:

"This is my impossible love story."

That was at that moment, in those days. When you gave me as a present the CD of the Swedish singer Agnes with the song that reads "Nothing is impossible," you broke up the impossibility and opened the door to this time of possibility.

When you wrote:

"May I have your love today or tomorrow?"

You couldn't have it "that today" but you left open the possibility of having it tomorrow. That day you weren't suspicious about tomorrow really coming true one day, and that that day is "today."

When you stated:

"If this feeling is inside me I will never let it go."

And you took the compromise as each day of your life you inevitably thought about me.

When you said:

"It is you the one I have been looking for day by day."

You made me truly believe in twin souls. You made me think about the possibility of having been together centuries ago in other lives. It is said that one chooses your parents before you are born and I came to this world before you. Maybe we agreed above there and it took you two years but you came following me. Were you looking for me? Take a rest. You have already found me.

When you wrote …

"I'm leaving for Europe. I don't know when I'm coming back."

It's just you were going to come back when it was the right time. Only when an angel pushed me and I called you.

When you explained …

"I will always remember you and love you."

You simply complied with your promise. The same way I did when I learnt to love you in silence during so many years until I found you again.

I adore you,
Clara.
♥

How many things Daniel had done for Clara to show her his love! How many modifications he had made in his life motivated by his eternal love for Clara.

What would Clara do to show him her love?

Clara trusted the forces of attraction. Now she knew, she understood that any dream can come true provided that she thought about it, that she believed in it, trusted it, and asked the universe for it.

Then, everything would go to her until she could reach what both of them wished. So, she decided to forge her own destiny; she decided to become the author of her own life ...

And that was how Clara started writing her love story.

Daniel and Clara currently live together. They spend some time in the northern hemisphere and some in the southern hemisphere. Their story inspires those who have lost hope. It shows the powerful strength of love. It teaches us to be alert to signs and to act in order to obtain what we want.

About the Author

Claudia Compagnucci has been a bilingual English teacher in Buenos Aires, Argentina, for the last thirty years. She also holds a degree in Management of Education USAL. She started writing in 2008 and took a coaching program course with the talented American author and coach Jack Canfield. Her knowledge and experience led her to start helping other people, mostly English teachers and educators who wanted to improve their performances and have a different perspective on their own lives. This led her to study as a postgraduate in Organizational Coaching at Universidad del Salvador USAL.

Today Claudia enjoys helping people through her writings and coaching courses, giving them the opportunity to find their inner wisdom to help them make spiritual progress and fill their lives with an abundance of love.

Find out more at www.claudiacompagnucci.com.

Bibliography

- Buscaglia, Leo. *Vivir, Amar y Aprender* (Living, Loving and Learning) Buenos Aires: Emecé Editores, S.A, 1987.
- Cooper, Diana. *Vislumbrando a Los Ángeles*. Buenos Aires, Argentina: Longseller, 1999.
- Chopra Deepak. *Sincrodestino*. (Synchrodestiny) Buenos Aires, Argentina: Alamah, Aguilar, Altea, Taurus, Alfaguara S.A de C.V. 2003–2007.
- Giddens, Anthony. *La Constitución de la Sociedad*. (The Constitution of Society) Teoría de la Estructuración prácticas sociales que ocurren en el espacio-tiempo. Bs As, Argentina: Amorrortu Editores, 1995.
- Hall, Edward. *The Silent Language*. New York, United States of America: An Anchor book published by Doubleday a division of Bantam Doubleday Dell Publishing Group Inc, 1959–1981.
- Parrado, Nando. *Milagro en Los Andes*. (Miracle in the Andes) Buenos Aires, Argentina: Editorial Planeta, 2006.
- Virgen de San Nicolás. http://www.virgen-de-san-nicolas.org/index.html

Other authors and musicians:

- ✓ Barlow, Josiah. 2005. "Angelfire" from the album "Power, Passion, Expression" www.josiahbarlow.com.
- ✓ Carlsson, Agnes. "Right Here, Right Now," "Nothing is Impossible."(P) & (C) Sony BMG Music Entertainment (Sweden) AB. Columbia Records, Printed in the United States, 2005. www.agnescarlsson.se
- ✓ Collins, Phil. "Another Day in Paradise" United States of America: Atlantic Records, WEA, 1989. United Kingdom: Virgin Records, 1989.
- ✓ Streisand, Barbara. "Woman in Love" Collection Greatest Hits-Artist (band). Writers: Barry Gibb, Robin Gibb. Miami, United States of America: Columbia Records, 1980.
- ✓ "El Hotel de Hielo en Suecia". "The Ice Hotel," Sweden) http://www.icehotel.com

Recommended authors and books:

- ✓ Canfield, Jack. *The Success Principles: How to Get From Where You Are to Where You Want to Be*. New York: Harper Collins Publishers, Inc., 2005.
- ✓ McTaggart, Lynne. *The Field: The Quest for the Secret Force of the Universe*. Great Britain: Harper Collins Publishers, 2002.
- ✓ Zancolli, Eduardo. *El Misterio de las Coincidencias: Una Aventura guiada por la Sincronicidad*. (The Mystery of Coincidences: An Adventure guided by Synchronicity). Buenos Aires: Editorial del Nuevo Extremo, 2003.

Printed in the United States
By Bookmasters